"You can't possibly expect that we're going to live together,"

Carly told him.

Josh realized she was quite disturbed about the idea. He brought his blue eyes directly in line with her gaze. "Well, you only inherited half this house. Besides, there are two bedrooms. And you don't have to worry. I know how to behave myself."

Carly had never thought that was an issue. She doubted that a man like Josh Spencer would ever make a play for her.

Without her realizing it, Carly's eyes dropped to his muscular chest. She stared at the way his shirt clung to his broad shoulders, and wondered what it would be like to spend an entire night being held by such strong arms.

"What would you like to do first?" Josh asked innocently, effectively interrupting Carly's thoughts. Quickly her eyes jumped to his face, but not before she blushed bright red.

Dear Reader,

This month we have a wonderful lineup of love stories for you, guaranteed to warm your heart on these chilly autumn nights.

Favorite author Terry Essig starts us off with love and laughter in this month's FABULOUS FATHERS title, *Daddy on Board*. Lenore Pettit knew her son, Tim, needed a father figure—but why did the boy choose her boss, Paul McDaniels? And how did Tim ever persuade her to let Paul take them all on a cross-country "family" vacation?

Those rugged men of the West always have a way of winning our hearts, as Lindsay Longford shows us in *The Cowboy and the Princess*. Yet, when devilishly handsome heartbreaker Hank Tyler meets Gillian Elliot, she seems to be the *only* woman alive immune to his charms! Or, is this clever "princess" just holding out to be Hank's bride?

Anne Peters winds up her FIRST COMES MARRIAGE trilogy with *Along Comes Baby*. When Ben Kertin finds Marcie Hillier, pregnant and penniless, he gallantly offers marriage. But Marcie longs for more than Ben's compassion—she wants to win his love.

Jayne Addison brings us a fun-filled Western romance in *Wild West Wife*. And don't miss Donna Clayton's *Fortune's Bride*—a surprise inheritance brings one woman unexpected love. And, in Laura Anthony's *Second Chance Family*, reunited lovers are given a new chance at happiness.

Happy Reading!

Anne Canadeo

Senior Editor

Please address questions and book requests to:
Silhouette Reader Service
U.S.: 3010 Walden Ave., P.O. Box 1325, Buffalo, NY 14269
Canadian: P.O. Box 609, Fort Erie, Ont. L2A 5X3

WILD WEST WIFE

Jayne Addison

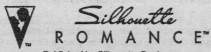

Silhouette
R O M A N C E™
Published by Silhouette Books
America's Publisher of Contemporary Romance

SILHOUETTE BOOKS

ISBN 0-373-19117-0

WILD WEST WIFE

Copyright © 1995 by Jane Atkin

This edition published by arrangement with Harlequin Books S.A.

® and TM are trademarks of Harlequin Books S.A., used under license.
Trademarks indicated with ® are registered in the United States Patent
and Trademark Office, the Canadian Trade Marks Office and in other
countries.

Printed in U.S.A.

JAYNE ADDISON

lives on the North Shore of Long Island with her husband, Jerry. Their three children, Steven, Andrew and Beth, are presently attending colleges away from home. Jayne finds that writing romance fiction is a great way to beat the empty-nest syndrome. When Jayne isn't writing, reading or on the phone, you can find her at her local video store checking out rentals. Needless to say, romance flicks are her favorites.

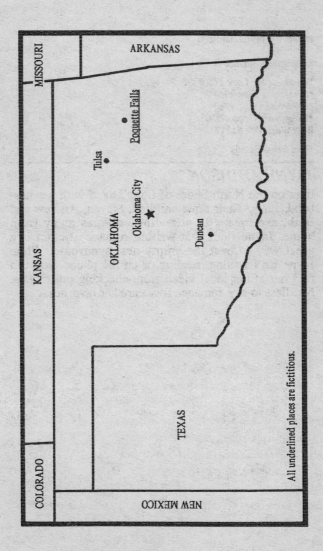

COLORADO

KANSAS

MISSOURI

ARKANSAS

OKLAHOMA

Tulsa

Poquette Falls

Oklahoma City

Duncan

TEXAS

NEW MEXICO

All underlined places are fictitious.

Prologue

Josh Spencer straightened in his chair, put down his drink and checked out his hand of poker. He was holding a pair of deuces, a lone red queen, a ten and a three.

He tossed a buck to the center of the table.

His friend Ben Keane grabbed some peanuts, washed them down with the last of his fourth can of beer, then met the first-round wager.

"Hey, I just realized tomorrow is the big day," Josh's other friend Paulie said, putting his dollar in. "I take that back. It's already tomorrow."

"Don't remind me," Josh muttered.

"I don't know why having a female partner has you all turned out," Ben commented, closing his cards, then fanning them open again for another look.

"I refuse to allow any female to have a say in any

part of my life,'' Josh responded tightly, discarding
the ten and three facedown, wishfully holding on to
the queen. Though they'd been playing for hours
in the mess hall of the bunkhouse, Josh had only won
a couple of hands.

"He's still got the 'I-was-once-married hangover
blues,''' Paulie bantered, parceling out two cards for
the two Josh had discarded.

"Right," Josh rejoined, taking note that his wish-
ful thinking hadn't paid off. He hadn't got a sister for
the queen and he hadn't got anything to add to the
deuces.

Ben put down a card and picked up a new one. He
looked at it, then looked over at Josh. "Did you marry
one of those give-me and get-me types?''

"That just about sums it up," Josh answered,
watching Paulie put down two cards of his own.

Paulie, his poker face firmly in place, raised his eyes
from his new hand. "So what are you going to do
about Bobby's niece?''

"Buy her out," Josh replied matter-of-factly, an-
teing up another buck.

Ben folded his hand, taking himself out of the
game. "What if she doesn't want to be bought out?''

"I can tell you that I'm not going to lay down and
play dead. If she doesn't want to be bought out, then
I'll just have to figure out another way to induce her
to leave." Josh eyed Paulie as the other man lifted a
five dollar bill from the pile he'd already won.

"You want to see me, it'll cost you." Paulie waved
the bill in the air.

Josh threw four more bucks on the table. "I'll take a look."

Paulie showed him a pair of tens.

"It's all yours." Josh shrugged loosely.

Paulie collected his winnings. "What do they say? Unlucky in cards, lucky in love."

"Yeah, right." Josh laughed. "I guess I'm just an exception to the rule."

"Where's she going to be staying?" Ben asked as they took their customary break between hands.

Josh took a swallow of beer. "According to the letter she sent me with her flight arrangements, she's under the impression that she'll be moving into her uncle's home."

"Where are you going to be staying?" Ben asked.

"I'm not moving out. I own half the place."

"So what's the game plan?" Paulie asked. "You looking to make her as uncomfortable as you can?"

"Whatever it takes to get her out of my hair." Josh stuck his fingers through his dark blond hair.

"I wonder what she looks like," Ben said.

"High-style New York chic." Josh replied. He'd already formed a picture of her in his mind. "Thinks she can cut any man off at the knees with just a look."

"I've got twenty that says she's short, dumpy and wears glasses." Paulie threw his opinion in.

"I say she's hot." Ben emphasized his theory with some exaggerated heavy breathing.

"*Thinks* she's hot," Josh quipped.

Ben sucked in his breath. "Short skirt, tight top. Oh, and real high heels."

"Cool it down." Josh grinned.

"Are we all in for twenty?" Paulie formalized the wager.

"I'm in," Ben replied.

Josh nodded his head. "It's a bet."

Chapter One

Josh braked behind a line of other cars jockeying to pull up in front of the arrival terminal. He spotted his reason for being at the airport, as he waited for his turn to park near the sidewalk. He figured the woman had to be Carly Gerard. She was the only female of the right age standing in front of the private airline that made the short connecting run between Tulsa and Poquotte Falls.

She was tall, though she wore low-heeled pumps. He couldn't tell much of anything about her shape, except that she didn't seem to be overweight. The short-sleeved boxy cream-colored suit she'd selected to travel in hung straight to just past her knees, too stiff to make any indentations on the way. She was speaking to a young male who had wheeled her three suitcases to the front of the terminal. From his position in the

car, Josh was unable to get a totally unobstructed view
of her face.

There was no missing her hair. Actually, the very
first thing he'd noticed about her was her thick, curly
carrot-red tresses. She had obviously made an effort
to keep the unruly mass neat with silver clips and a
twirly kind of topknot. It hadn't stayed under control. Tendrils of wavy red hair had squirmed free to
wiggle against her cheeks and dangle down the nape of
her neck. The twirl of hair on top of her head, which
had no doubt started out centered, now dipped to one
side.

The other cars in front of Josh began to move, giving him access to pull up in front of her. The young
male who had removed her suitcases from the dolly
was just walking away, pocketing the tip she'd given
him.

Turning from her luggage, Carly noticed the Jeep
with the words Wild West Show stenciled across the
hood. In a matter of a half second, Carly's hazel eyes
shifted to the cowboy getting out from behind the
wheel. He had on tight jeans and a beige oxford shirt
with cuffs rolled halfway up his forearms. It was more
his dark Stetson, angled low on his brow, and his not-
just-for-show roughly scuffed boots that gave him a
one-tough-hombre appearance. Carly was mesmer-
ized as he approached her. He was the first real-life
cowboy she'd ever seen.

As Josh moved towards Carly, he saw that her skirt
was badly rumpled and that there was a stain just be-
low the line of her jacket. His blue-eyed gaze slid back
up to her face. He expected to find some freckles but

her skin was flawless. From what he could tell, she didn't use makeup. If she'd even had lipstick on at the start of the day, it was now gone. Her mouth, he realized with male interest, was nice and full. She was pretty. Really pretty. But not the type guys would try to pick up. She didn't give off that come-and-get-me signal. She wasn't voguish or chic, either. What kind of feminine game did she play?

"I'm Josh Spencer," he said, extending his hand.

Carly's heart was palpitating. She always had trouble acting breezy and composed around any male within the vicinity of her own age. Especially when they were good-looking. This one, who had just announced himself as her new partner, was not only just good-looking, he was unbelievably sexy.

"I'm Carly Gerard." It took her a second to place her hand in the one he was holding out to her. Clint Eastwood at his very best had nothing on *this* cowboy.

"Get in. I'll get your luggage," Josh said, after a brief hand-to-hand contact.

Carly thought she should offer to assist him by grabbing an end of one of her suitcases. Her luggage was heavy. But before she had the chance to make the offer, he'd already lifted the first suitcase. She watched him place it on the back seat and looked dubiously at the Jeep. She'd never been in one before. The thought of riding in a vehicle without doors made her more anxious and jittery than she already was.

Josh regarded her after he settled himself behind the wheel. "Is something the matter?" he asked, fixing his seat belt.

"No. Everything's fine." Carly tried for some affected ease. She did push a little forward against the seat belt she'd already hooked in place around herself—just to test how well it held.

Josh took off his hat, ran fingers through his heavy blondish-brown hair, then set the Stetson back on his head. "You don't look like you're comfortable."

"I'm perfectly comfortable." Doubling her effort, Carly did a little blasé hand motion for him. Her posture remained rigid and her heartbeat continued to accelerate. She didn't know what she felt most uncomfortable and anxious about—being in his company or being in his company in the doorless Jeep.

As Josh turned the motor over, Carly dropped her gaze and caught sight of the stain on her skirt. She'd known it was there, but she hadn't had it on her mind again until just now. If she'd had a blouse on under her suit jacket, she would have folded her jacket on her lap. Instead, Carly placed the pouch of her natural leather shoulder bag on the spot. She didn't want to think about the first impression she'd made on him. Even at her very best, she wouldn't expect to make much of one at all.

Josh steered the Jeep away from the curb. "How was your flight?"

"There was some turbulence on the way to Tulsa. The woman next to me grabbed hold of my arm as I was drinking a glass of wine." She didn't care to let on that she'd embarrassingly panicked when the plane hit an air pocket. Thankfully, she'd been drinking white wine, rather than red.

Josh nodded casually. "I sat next to a woman once who repeated 'oh, my' for three hours."

Carly gave him what she hoped was an insouciant smile. Even before she'd spilled wine on herself and tried to wash it out, she'd been dismayed at how badly her new outfit had wrinkled. The saleswoman had said that the linen-looking material was a synthetic fiber that didn't crease.

"Fly often?" Josh asked, making small talk.

"Occasionally." Carly used a sophisticated tone. This was the third time she'd ever flown, and the first time she'd flown alone. She'd gone to Walt Disney World when she was a senior in high school. She'd flown to Bermuda with her two roommates last year.

Former roommates, Carly corrected in her mind, but still close friends. She'd moved out of the midtown apartment she'd shared with Jessie Marlow and Christy Young once the notice of her inheritance settled in. She still couldn't believe she'd become an entrepreneur. She felt as if she'd taken a quantum leap into someone else's life.

Josh glanced her way again.

"Were you and my uncle partners for long?" She asked, taking in how blue his eyes were just before she lost his gaze. The first three buttons of his shirt were undone, allowing her a glimpse of his dark blond chest hair. She'd never been more aware of a man's masculinity in her entire life.

"Almost two years." Josh eased the Jeep into the flow of some light traffic that yielded onto a highway.

"Were you working for my uncle before you became his partner?" Carly rubbed her hands up and down her arms trying to calm her nerves. It was hard for her to concentrate on her composure. She was feeling even less safe in the Jeep now that they were on the highway.

"No. I meet your uncle in a bar one night in Tulsa. We got to talking and drinking. He told me that he owned a Wild West Show. He said he could use a partner. I went to see the show...thought to myself 'what the hell,' and I bought in."

"Just like that?" Carly looked at him incredulously.

"Just like that." Josh's gaze locked with hers. "I guess you're not impulsive."

"No." Carly thought it was just as well that he knew that about her up front. "What were you doing before you joined my uncle?"

"Just doing what cowboys do," Josh answered lackadaisically.

"What do cowboys do?" Carly inquired, then thought the question might have sounded a little flirty. Flirting with Josh was not something she would do. She couldn't even see herself entertaining the notion of flirting with him.

Josh had no idea what cowboys did. What *he'd* been doing was what every other lawyer in his large, prestigious New York City law firm did. Working himself up to partnership status. He had made it happen only to discover that the accomplishment felt nothing more than materialistic and hollow. There he had been starched, stain-resistant and empty. Very empty.

"Cowboys ride rodeos. Herd cattle. Drift around. Cowboys spend a lot of time looking for themselves," was the answer he gave her.

Carly personally related to the last part of his response. She'd thought she knew who she was—a bookkeeper for a small garment company in Manhattan. She hadn't been unhappy with her life. She'd felt secure. She'd never had an occasion to meet any challenges head-on, not counting a couple of blind dates that Jessie and Christy had talked her into. Then the inheritance came. Suddenly she wasn't who she thought she was. Now, she was out looking for herself.

"Have you found yourself?" Carly thought she should know if he intended to stick around as her partner.

"It feels that way." The Wild West Show was as corny as anything he could have imagined. But it had turned out to be the cure to what ailed him. He was having the time of his life.

"I expect there's a lot to manage in this kind of business." Carly tried to keep from worrying about being able to hold up her end. She was a fast learner. At least she had that going for her.

"It's not the kind of business you can just sit back and manage." Josh fashioned her a look with his cobalt-blue eyes. "Do you ride?"

"Ride what?" Carly unconsciously crossed her legs, forgetting about holding herself rigidly to her seat.

"A horse." He'd figured that since she'd chosen to wear her skirt so long, she had knobby knees. Now, with her skirt hiked up some, he could see that there was nothing at all wrong with her knees, or her legs for that matter. Josh contemplated whether she'd ever tried to be deliberately provocative, but couldn't come up with an image to match the thought.

"I've never been on a horse." Carly swallowed nervously.

"I'll get you up on one first thing. You'll be a regular cowgirl before you know it." He tossed her a wink.

Carly thought of how she sometimes tripped over herself just walking. She could just imagine what would happen if she tried to get on a horse.

"How about acting?" He held her eyes for a second. "Have you ever done any acting?"

"Acting?" Carly's voice squeaked. She cleared her throat.

"This *is* show business."

Carly realized she hadn't given any thought at all to the "show" part of the business. She could hear her mother and father arguing with her not to burn her bridges. To go out first and take a long look, see what the ranch was all about.

Had she listened? No. This was her chance to be more than she'd ever thought she was going to be. Though an actress and a cowgirl were not what she had envisioned. She'd seen herself in an office, holding meetings, directing promotional campaigns, doing lunch...

"About acting—" Carly began.

"Hey, I can see you're worried about it. Don't be. We get some hecklers once in a while, but not that often."

Oh, God! Carly felt her heart jumping all over the place.

"Is there a guy back in New York?" Josh asked, changing the subject.

If her mind hadn't still been on horses and acting, Carly would have answered, "No one in particular," which would have sounded better than just... "No."

She did anticipate that Mr. Right would eventually come along. She saw him as pleasant enough to look at, quite a little shy. He'd have a decent job and together they'd work to save for a small house in the suburbs. And they'd have three children. Anyway, she wasn't planning to panic until she hit thirty. And she still had three years to go. Right now she had other things to panic about. *Maybe* she could learn to ride a horse, but acting... in front of an audience...

Carly made an attempt to redirect her thoughts, at least for a moment. "Are you married?"

"I was married once." Josh accelerated to pass the car in front of him. "Have you ever been married?" he asked.

"No." Carly wondered what had gone wrong with his marriage. She certainly wasn't going to inquire.

There was a long stretch of silence before Carly realized they weren't making conversation. She'd been busy listening to her nervous system telling her that she'd bitten off more than she could chew.

"My uncle was married once," Carly said, trying to fill in the silence. "According to the information that I received from his lawyer, he never married again. I didn't even know that I had an uncle in Oklahoma. He was my father's brother—the black sheep of the family. My father first told me about him after I was contacted about my inheritance. The last time my father saw Bob, I was six months old. My father had named him my godfather when I was born." Was she rattling?

Josh had wondered why Bob Gerard had singled her out as his heir. Given the fact that the man had no children of his own, it made sense that he'd left half his ranch to his goddaughter.

Carly continued. "I suppose there's more to it, but the way my father explained it, his brother had gone out to buy a newspaper one morning and never returned. He called my father a few days later. Dad was furious with him. Not only had Uncle Bob walked out on his wife, but he'd also left Dad high and dry. He had been my father's partner in his plumbing business."

Josh's mind drifted back to the morning that he'd woken up and realized just how unhappy he was. He'd looked at his wife, still sleeping beside him. They'd been married for less than a year and she'd already decided that she knew him better than he knew himself. She had his whole life mapped out for him. Congressman Spencer. Senator Spencer. Esteem, money and power. What had ever happened to the for-richer-or-poorer part of their wedding vows?

"Your uncle was unhappy with everything in his life at the time," Josh told her. "He couldn't see any other way out, except to make a clean break. He did regret the split with your father. I think your father would like to know that."

"I'm sure Dad would like knowing that," Carly confirmed, relieved to be picking up a sensitivity in Josh Spencer's personality. Once she made him understand that she was too shy to do any acting, he'd be willing to compromise. She felt better already. Better enough to ask a question she probably wouldn't have otherwise asked.

"Did you leave your wife the same way my uncle did?"

Josh gave her half a grin. "No. I didn't go out to buy a newspaper."

Carly saw a sharp turn in the road coming up. She held her breath and gripped her seat. She let out her breath after he'd maneuvered the turn not even jogging her as he passed a motel at the bend.

Just about five minutes later, Carly spotted a sign advertising that the approach to The Greatest Wild West Show in America was coming up. Excitement bubbling, Carly read four more signs, each about a mile apart, each a little larger than the one before it.

Then they were there. And there was no missing The Greatest Wild West Show in America. It was smack-dab on the highway.

Josh pulled off the road. He braked, left the motor running and jumped out of the Jeep. He unlocked a gate with a key that he pulled out of his jeans pocket. After pushing the gate open, he got back inside the Jeep. Josh steered through the gate, stopped again and got out to close the gate.

"How do people get in with the gate locked?" Carly asked, once he was driving again.

"We're not open to the public today. We're open Wednesday through Sunday."

"Oh," Carly said, glad that it was Monday. She'd have the rest of today and all of tomorrow to acclimatize herself to her surroundings. Carly knew she was going to need longer than that to acclimatize herself to her partner.

Josh drove through the opening of a large canvas tent that looked like the covering to a circus, crossed a parking lot, which wasn't blacktopped but just sparsely flattened grass, then past a semicircle of stadium benches. In front of the benches, in a squared-off area of dirt, was what looked to Carly like a Hollywood set for a Western ghost town. A small Western ghost town.

"There isn't very much to it," Carly said, making a drastic adjustment to her expectations. She'd been imagining a miniature Disney World. Her imagination had been way off.

Josh didn't miss the look of disappointment on her face. He recalculated the offer he was going to make to buy her out. It didn't look as if it was going to take all that much. "I'll get you settled, then you can come back and look around."

Carly kept turning her head from side to side as Josh drove behind additional billboards backing the ghost town. She saw some barn structures, a fenced pasture, two log cabins—one rather large, the other much smaller.

Josh brought the Jeep to a halt in front of the porch of the smaller log cabin. He turned off the ignition and got out of the vehicle. Carly looked down at the muddy ground as he came around to her.

"I can lift you over it if you want," Josh said, standing in the mud with his Western boots. He didn't think she'd want to be lifted up, but it had rained pretty hard the day before and the ground was very soggy.

"I can manage," Carly said quickly as she unfastened her seat belt. She stretched one leg out, trying to get to the first step of the porch while at the same time reaching out for the railing.

She got her foot on the first step, but was unable to get her hand on the railing. Had he not gripped her from behind as she tried for balance, she would have toppled sideways into the mud. As it was she broke the heel of her shoe in her effort to right herself.

"You shouldn't have stopped me from being gallant," Josh said teasingly against her ear. His hands had discovered that she had a waist. A firm, small waist. He was also taking in the sweet scent of her hair, and feeling a crazy urge to blow against a wisp just in front of his mouth.

Carly could feel her whole body becoming flushed. She had her back to him, his hands still on her waist, and she was standing lopsided in the mud.

"Sorry I ruined your moment," Carly replied, shocking herself by bantering. She didn't banter. She thought of herself as too serious-minded to banter.

"You've also ruined your shoes," Josh said lightly as he let go of her. He wasn't expecting her to be sassy. She didn't look at all like a street-smart type. More of a librarian. That was the impression she'd given him up until now. Then again, for all he knew, that impression could be as phony as a two-dollar bill. Females could be very adept at getting a guy to think whatever it was they wanted them to.

"Half the time we're walking around knee-deep in mud out here," Josh added as they moved onto the porch. "I hope you have boots with you."

Carly nodded her head. Though she didn't have Western boots, she had her good dress boots, and boots that she wore when it rained. Just how often did it rain around here, anyway?

Josh kicked off his boots outside the door to the cabin. Carly followed suit, stepping out of her ruined muddy shoes, then adjusting her stance now that both her feet were level.

When he opened the door she followed him inside.

"So... this is my uncle's home," Carly said, looking around. They'd entered directly into the living room. It was clean, tidy and without any frills. The couch was covered in a Southwestern print. The armchairs were upholstered in a terra-cotta shade, the same color as the rug in the center of the room. Carly loved the stone fireplace that was built across an entire wall. She thought the room was charming.

"Your uncle's home and mine." Josh dropped his bombshell on her.

"Excuse me?" Carly's narrow face was all eyes. "I inherited my uncle's home."

"You inherited half of it," Josh said easily.

"Half of it," Carly repeated.

"There's two bedrooms. You don't have to worry. I know how to behave myself."

Carly hadn't thought that was an issue. Not for one moment. She was no fool. She knew that no man who looked like Josh Spencer would ever make a play for her. She didn't attract many males to begin with.

Without her realizing it, Carly's eyes dropped to the zipper of his jeans. Quickly, her eyes jumped to his face. "You can't possibly expect that we're going to live together."

It was obvious to Josh that she was quite disturbed about that idea. It was a start.

Josh brought his blue eyes directly in line with her green-flecked hazel gaze. He realized they were almost the same height, even though he was a little more than six feet. "There isn't anyplace else you can stay on the grounds. I don't think you want to stay in the bunkhouse. Some of the men who work the show live there. You won't have any privacy at all."

Carly chewed her full bottom lip. Where was his gallantry now? Couldn't he bunk in with the men until they figured this out? "Aren't there any women working here?"

"Sure, and there are other men. They come and go just like they would at any job."

Carly could hear her mother saying, "You can't run out there like a chicken with its head cut off." "I'll stay in a motel for now. I think we passed one on the road."

"The Red Star Motel is about five miles back, but you don't have a car." Josh winged it. "How are you going to travel back and forth? I'd offer to drive you and pick you up, but I promised one of the men the Jeep tonight. He won't be back until Wednesday morning." Josh figured he'd give Denny Robbins the Jeep and a couple of bucks. That would take care of that issue.

"Isn't there any other car around?" She couldn't fault him now. He was trying to be accommodating. This was his home, too. She didn't have the right to expect him to move out.

Josh wasn't about to mention his motorcycle. All the guys living on the grounds had bikes. They kept them in a shed when they weren't being used. Josh was certain that if he asked Paulie, Ben and even Billy Jack not to take their bikes out in sight of her, they'd cooperate. He didn't see her hanging in more than a couple of days, if that long.

Josh shook his head. "Look, why don't we leave our living arrangement aside for the moment. I'm sure you're anxious to check everything out. I'll bring in your suitcases. You can put on your boots, and we can take a walk around." He didn't anticipate her making a deal with him until she'd fully explored what she'd inherited.

"I don't feel up to taking a walk right now." She needed some time alone to think.

"Are you hungry?" he asked.

"No." Carly's gaze drifted away from his. Maybe it had been a stupid idea to burn her bridges, but she had. Not only had she trained someone to take over her job, but she'd also found someone to pick up her end of the lease. The apartment she'd shared was one of those rare finds in New York. The location was great and the rent was actually down-to-earth. Of course, she could still go back and start all over again.

Carly moaned silently. Where was her gumption? She had to have some gumption somewhere. Was she going to run at the first challenge she met?

"What would you like to do?" Josh asked.

"I don't know." Carly sighed to herself. "I guess I could take a look at the books." At least that was something familiar to her.

"Do you know how to look at a set of books?"

"I'm a bookkeeper. I've also taken some accounting courses."

"Your uncle did the paperwork. He kept everything in the den."

Carly trailed after Josh as he led the way. The den was just through a door off the living room. Carly moved to the desk and sat in the chair behind it while Josh walked to a row of file cabinets. There wasn't much furniture in the small room. Her eyes went directly to the stuffed head of a moose mounted on one of the walls. Feeling her stomach start to turn, Carly quickly redirected her gaze.

Josh put a shoe box down on the desk. He removed the lid to reveal that it was filled with scraps of paper. Carly looked down, then up. "These are the books?" She was horrified.

"Your uncle had his own system, when he got around to it." Josh opened a drawer of the desk just at Carly's side. He took out a black and white notebook. "We have an accountant who comes out from town once a month. I asked him to come out tomorrow to give you a rundown of the business's worth."

Carly nodded studiously, opening the black and white notebook to a bunch of scribbling.

"You don't really want to bother looking through this, do you?" He didn't see any point to it. She was going to be able to find out everything she needed to know about the business tomorrow.

"If it's okay with you, I would like to look through some of these papers." Carly closed the notebook and brought her attention back to the shoe box. Even with her reading glasses, Carly didn't think she'd be able to make out much of anything in the notebook.

"It's okay with me." Josh shrugged. "I'll bring your suitcases in. I've got a few things to do. I'll check back on you a little later."

After he left the room Carly took her reading glasses out of her shoulder bag. She put them on, and squinted at the moose head hanging above the desk. She tried very hard not to feel a symbolic relationship to it.

Chapter Two

"It's time for you to put that away," Josh told Carly, coming back into the den after giving her less than an hour to look over the papers. "Dinner is almost ready over at the bunkhouse." He'd worked out what he'd needed to with the guys and felt it was safe to introduce Carly to the men who lived on the ranch.

Carly cast Josh a stunning, unreserved smile that had cost her father a fortune in orthodontist bills. She hadn't got anywhere at all with the papers in the shoe box, but she had accomplished something.

"What's that smile for?" Josh smiled back without thinking.

Carly beamed. "I made a reservation at the Red Star Motel, *and* I found a car service in town that will drive me back and forth. I told them I'd call when I was ready to leave here."

She took the wind right out of his sails, walloping him with her resourcefulness. "I didn't know there was a car service around."

Carly smiled again. "I was thinking that maybe we could work some kind of financial arrangement through the business that would cover me after I find a place to rent. Sort of an exchange on the house. I'll buy a secondhand car on my own."

"Let's talk about it after we eat." This thing was getting out of hand right before his very eyes. Josh carelessly ran strong fingers through his uncovered hair. "I'll show you where your suitcases are."

"Thank you for being willing to drive me back and forth," Carly said, walking with Josh. "I really appreciate how nice you're being to me." She couldn't get over what a terrific guy he was. Terrific, good-looking, sexy and sensitive. The combination made Carly's head swim.

Great! Josh groaned inwardly, slicing off his guilty conscience before it took hold. His eyes lit on her briefly and caught another smile aimed his way. Quickly he averted his gaze. She *did* have a fantastic smile.

"I'm starved," Carly said brightly. "I didn't realize how hungry I was until you mentioned dinner. Who does the cooking?" She was pleased with the way she was conducting herself with him. Carly considered that eventually she might even be able to take his incredible male pulchritude in stride.

Not looking at her, Josh answered offhandedly, "Gabby Hale. His first name is really Art, but everyone calls him Gabby."

She could see her suitcases now as they reached the threshold of one of the bedrooms. It was a large room with a double bed. Decorated in a Southwestern motif, it was just as warm and inviting as the living room.

"I won't be long," Carly said and closed the door as Josh turned back to the living room.

Keeping her word, she came out of the bedroom ten minutes later. She'd tidied her hair some, lifting most of the strands off the nape of her neck, and catching a number of the errant wisps that had been swaggering against her checks. She'd straightened the top-knot as best she could without taking time to redo it, not wanting dinner to be held up on her account.

Distracted as Josh was by the turn of events, his eyes still appraisingly perused her length. She'd put on a tailored plaid shirt, tucking it loosely into jeans that were on the baggy side. She'd stuffed the legs of her jeans into flat-heeled black rubber boots. She was even thinner than he'd realized.

"You'd better take a jacket," Josh said in passing. "The temperature drops pretty low at night."

Feeling wonderfully swamped with his show of concern, Carly left Josh to go back into the bedroom. She returned moments later with a dark green wool blazer over her arm. She could hardly believe her luck at getting Josh Spencer for a partner.

The sun was still out, as it was the middle of June and only six-thirty. The walk to the bunkhouse was short, and Carly and Josh easily traversed the mud and some puddles.

Josh didn't bother trying to make conversation. He was busy thinking, hoping for inspiration. Exasperation was all that surfaced. He hadn't expected that she'd so easily eliminate the first obstacle he'd thrown in her path.

He shot her a sidelong glance and thought of the smile she'd given him. A guy could be devastated by that smile of hers.

Carly was in her own world. She'd met her first real challenge, and she was feeling the sweet reward of success.

Outside the bunkhouse, they wiped the mud off their boots on a square of hemp, Josh held the door open for Carly to enter, then directed her toward the mess hall. She heard the raucous noise of talking before she saw any faces. There were four men seated at a long table—a number of chairs unoccupied. A fifth was stirring a pot on a commercial-sized stove.

The chatter ended as soon as Carly and Josh appeared. Carly took in the scene before her, breathing in the cooking odors, heavy with onions and garlic. She didn't like the way all eyes were curiously assessing her. Unconsciously, Carly took a step closer to Josh.

The man at the stove broke the quiet. "So, you're the niece." He smiled, crinkling up an already crinkled sun-leathered face as he walked over to her. His attitude was energetic and alert. "Howdy, little gal. The name's Art, but everyone around these here parts calls me Gabby."

Carly returned his smile. It was the first time in her life she'd been called little. She'd always been tall and gawky. Even way back in grade school, she'd towered over the other girls, and miserably over all the boys.

The equation hadn't changed all that much during high school.

"I'm very pleased to meet you," Carly said, shaking hands. She idly tried to guess his age. He could have been anywhere from fifty to seventy. The sturdiness of his physique belied the wrinkled appearance of his skin. He was obviously older than any of the other men in the room. Like Josh, the others looked to be in their late twenties or early thirties.

Josh kept his gaze on Carly. He wasn't certain, but he thought her eyes had got brighter at Gabby's welcome. He'd never seen eyes quite the color of hers.

The other men had got to their feet and formed a line. Josh did the honors, finding himself mentally approving the way she was holding herself straight, tall and receptive.

Carly could hear her mother's voice saying, "Don't slouch." Lord help me, Carly thought, heart hammering, her throat dry.

Denny Robbins, dressed in jeans and a tight-fitting black T-shirt that matched his dark curly hair, was introduced first. "Pleased to meet you, Ms. Gerard," he drawled.

"It's Carly." It was clear to her that Denny Robbins knew he was exceptionally good-looking. Carly didn't disagree, but she didn't feel any personal attraction. That surprised her. One on one, Denny Robbins was even better-looking than Josh Spencer.

Carly was then introduced to Paulie Mitchell, Ben Keane and finally Billy Jack Guthrie. All three men were attractive in their own way. Of the four, Carly was immediately attuned to Billy Jack. She recognized a kindred spirit. He seemed as shy as she was. Discounting Denny Robbins, Carly had a feeling that she could develop an easy relationship with each of them. It made her wonder about her inherent shyness.

"Ladies first," Gabby said, holding out a chair at the table.

Carly placed her blazer on the back of the wood chair and then sat. She was glad that Josh took the seat to her right. She was also pleased that Billy Jack was directly opposite her.

"First time in Oklahoma?" Denny asked, drawing Carly's attention.

"Yes," she responded politely to the man seated next to Billy Jack. Carly found herself thinking that she'd be much more discomfited in the company of all these men if it wasn't for Josh.

Josh, who was following the byplay, saw Denny fixing to crank on the well-worked charm he dished out to the opposite sex. That part of Denny's personality annoyed Josh suddenly.

Gabby brought a big pot of stew to the table, then went back for a large bowl of mashed potatoes. "I'm going to get some meat on your bones, little gal," he declared, after spooning out a heaping portion of stew and potatoes on a plate and setting it down in front of her.

"This is too much for me," Carly objected nicely, placing one hand to her stomach.

"You just keep eating, little gal." Gabby kept dishing out servings.

Full plates passed from one side of the table to the other. Each male accepted his in turn.

"I imagine you'll want to see something more of Oklahoma besides Poquotte Falls." Denny slanted Carly a smile. "I'd be happy to take you around. Show you Tulsa and Oklahoma City."

"I think I'm going to be pretty busy here for quite some time," Carly answered courteously, putting her fork to a mound of mashed potatoes.

Carly's remark about being here for some time rolled off of Josh. He was more concerned at the moment with Denny's maneuver to try for some time alone with her. Josh felt his annoyance getting the better of him. Was there any woman Denny didn't think he could get his hands on?

"I understand that you didn't know your uncle at all," Gabby said, while they were eating.

"No." Carly leaned forward.

"Great guy, your uncle," Gabby chattered. "Loved his poker games. He'd drive into Tulsa to play for big hands. He hardly ever won, but it never stopped him."

"Remember the night we got together and tried losing to him?" Paulie asked with a smile on his rugged face. He hadn't taken his sunglasses off indoors. The lenses were as dark as his hair.

"Yeah, and he lost anyway," Ben answered, pushing a mop of pale blond hair off his forehead only to have it fall forward again.

"Best Buffalo Bill this show's ever going to see," Gabby said between mouthfuls. "Wait till you see the show, little gal. You're going to get yourself a thrill."

Carly smiled. "Are you in the show?"

Gabby shook his head. "I've got enough to do with the cooking and cleaning up. Let me tell you, cowboys can be slobs."

"Who you calling a slob?" The kidding question came from Paulie.

"You're the biggest of them all," Gabby replied, and turned to Carly. "Paulie is our Butch Cassidy and Ben is the Sundance Kid."

"What part do you play?" Carly asked Billy Jack, wanting to draw him out.

"I don't do much of a part." Billy Jack gave Carly only half a look. He had very straight medium brown hair, light brown eyes, a small gap between his front teeth and an oh-shucks kind of manner. "I'm just one of the Wild Bunch in Cassidy and the Kid's gang."

Gabby continued holding court. "Denny is our Jesse James. That is, when he bothers showing up. Half the time we have to send out a posse looking for him. Josh fills in as Jesse James when Denny isn't around."

Chewing a large bite of meat, Josh was thinking to himself that the next time Denny pulled one of his disappearing acts, it was going to be his last. Josh wasn't feeling loose about Denny's lack of work ethic right now. In fact, he was just itching for Denny not to come back with the Jeep Wednesday morning.

Carly was romantically picturing Josh as Jesse James. She didn't have to stretch her imagination at all. Her mind found its own course.

"Josh is our Wild Bill Hickok as well," Gabby was saying. "Does a right fine job of it, too."

"You're going to have me blushing," Josh quipped, taking a turn to joke with Gabby.

Carly brought her eyes to Josh, smiling her amusement at his retort.

Josh didn't think his remark was that pithy, but he had nothing against the idea that she'd thought so.

"I don't think I can do any acting," Carly said, speaking to Gabby after she'd chewed and swallowed. "I don't even know how to ride a horse, and I know I'd die if someone heckled me."

"Heckled you?" Gabby grinned. "We've never had anyone heckle anyone yet. If you have a mind to try some of the skits, you won't have to ride a horse."

Carly looked at Josh. She was certain that he knew she was staring at him, but he didn't glance her way. Carly distinctly remembered him mentioning they got hecklers in the audience every so often.

"Hey, Josh," Gabby said. "Remember how Bobby used to call you Slick when he was looking to get your goat?"

Josh's breathing had already taken a pause. Now his whole body tensed. He tried to signal Gabby with his eyes not to go any further with the subject.

"Bobby? Is that my Uncle Bob?" Carly asked.

"Right." Gabby reached for a roll to mop up the gravy on his plate.

"Why did he call you Slick?" Carly directed her question to Josh.

"It was just a joke between us." Josh kept his eyes focused on his plate, though it was almost empty.

Gabby finished his roll. "Your uncle called him Slick because most people think of lawyers as being slick. Josh was a high-priced lawyer before he hitched up with us.''

''A lawyer?'' Carly's expression turned puzzled.

Josh saw the confusion on Carly's face from the corner of his eye, and took a deep breath.

Gabby smiled at Carly. ''Didn't Josh tell you he practiced law in New York City? Heard it was a real big firm.'' The older man slapped his knee. ''Hey, I just realized you two are both from New York. That gives you something in common right off. It's good for partners to have things in common.''

Carly tried to figure out in her mind why Josh had lied to her. She considered that he might have thought she'd be more impressed that he was a cowboy rather than a New York lawyer. Only that didn't make any sense. Why would he even want to impress her?

She thought again about the point he'd made about hecklers. The thought skittered around in her head getting nowhere.

''Well, I'm going to be taking off,'' Denny said, getting to his feet, his eyes set on Carly. ''Sure I can't talk you into a couple of days in Tulsa?''

Carly shook her head. ''Thank you for the offer, though.''

''Anyone for seconds?'' Gabby asked. ''Come on, little gal. You've got to eat more than that.''

Carly looked down at her plate, which was still half-full. She hadn't realized she'd stopped eating, but knew she was no longer hungry.

''I'll take some more,'' Ben piped up.

Gabby snickered comically. ''Ain't you got legs? You know where the stove is.''

Josh put his fork down and cast a careful glance at Carly. She didn't allow him eye contact. "Would you like to go back to the house?" he asked.

Carly nodded her head woodenly. "Dinner was delicious," she told Gabby. "I'll eat more next time when I'm not so tired."

"How about coffee?" Gabby asked in a rush. "I've got a pot on."

Josh answered before Carly had the chance to reply. "She's had a long flight. What she needs is a good night's sleep."

Carly took over for herself. "Thank you for everything. Thank you all for being so welcoming."

Paulie and Ben gave Josh quick interested looks, and then smiled their good-nights to Carly. Billy Jack gave a nod of his head.

"See you tomorrow," Gabby said, getting the last word in as Carly and Josh made their way to the door.

Outside the bunkhouse the sky was turning from a chalky yellow to a silver blue. There was a chill in the air.

"Put your jacket on," Josh said, feeling a slight breeze at the back of his shirt.

"I'm not cold," Carly answered sharply, suppressing a shiver. There was no getting away from it. He had lied to her. She was all tense about it.

Josh stopped in his tracks. Without giving her any warning, he took her blazer off her arm, put the jacket around her shoulders and began to walk again. Carly didn't put her arms through the sleeves, but she let the jacket stay over her shoulders. Her heart was racing wildly.

Out of habit, Josh kicked off his boots when they reached the door to the cabin. When Carly bent over to tackle her own boots. Josh squatted down so their eyes were level. "Lean against the house. I'll give you a hand."

"I can do it myself."

Josh straightened up and watched her. She struggled some, but she got the boots off without any mishap. When she finished she tossed her head almost belligerently at him.

Once inside the darkened living room, Josh hit the switch that turned on a couple of lamps. "Let's sit down." Josh remained standing, waiting for her to acquiesce.

Carly stepped ahead of him, selecting one of the chairs. Josh took the couch. There was a rectangular wood coffee table between them. Nicks and scratches on the surface.

In strained silence, Carly watched Josh rub his temples, as if he had a headache and wasn't feeling well. She heard him swallow—even saw his Adam's apple move. After a long few minutes, he slouched against the cushions, one arm carelessly slung on the back of the couch. "I know you're wondering why I didn't tell you I was a lawyer... am a lawyer."

"Why did you lie?" Carly crossed her arms tightly in front of herself. Her hands got hidden within the blazer still over her shoulders.

"I figured that your knowing I was a lawyer would have you thinking I was going to try and pull a fast one on you," Josh answered truthfully.

"A fast one?" Carly let him see how perplexed she was before she lowered her gaze. Her defenses, not strong to begin with, were extremely low.

Josh regarded the way she'd hunched into herself. Her hair had come loose again, and curls fell onto her cheeks. He hadn't wanted this conversation to take the direction it had.

Squaring his shoulders, he said, "I want to buy you out. I'm prepared to make you a generous offer—more than your shares are worth. You'll see that for yourself after you meet with the accountant."

"You don't want me as a partner?" Carly floundered with this possibility that she hadn't even considered.

Josh decided to lay it out for her there plain and simple. "I don't want a female partner."

It was all starting to make sense to her now. His talk about hecklers and about her needing to ride a horse. He'd been trying to scare her off. "What do you have against a female partner?" Carly asked stiffly.

"That's immaterial."

But it wasn't immaterial as far as Carly was concerned. "Tell me."

"There isn't anything glamorous about this lifestyle, Carly." He tried reasoning with her.

"I'm sure you came here from a much more glamorous life-style than I did. I'm not looking for glamour."

Carly thought about how she'd naively thanked him earlier for being so nice to her. His show of courtesy had all been pretense—obviously something to do with deterring her from thinking he was pulling a "fast one." Carly couldn't recall ever having been so hurt.

"What are you looking for?" He wasn't about to let another woman come along and mess up his life. His heart might not be in the line of fire, but his livelihood was.

"That's immaterial." Carly's emotions crested from hurt to anger. "I have no intention of selling out. I can learn to do anything that you do here. You don't have to worry about me doing my fair share just because I'm female."

"I'm not worried about you doing your share," Josh countered flippantly. "This just isn't going to work out. I know when you think about it, you'll realize it yourself. Being out here is far afield from living in New York."

"You seem to have gotten used to it, coming from New York," Carly retaliated, surprised at her commanding tone of voice.

"I'm a guy. There's a big difference." Her stubbornness had him rankled. She was a fish out of water. Couldn't she see that?

Carly raised her chin even higher. She wanted to say something to really set him in his place. "In case you haven't noticed, women are doing all sorts of jobs these days. We're even going to make it to the White House one day."

Josh looked into Carly's stormy face. His own annoyance was evident. "Fine. You want to hang in and show me that you can do whatever I do, go to it." She might not be willing to see it right now, but the futility of this arrangement was going to hit her.

Carly felt like it was high noon at the O.K. Corral. "I intend to do exactly that." Getting up from her chair, Carly marched into the kitchen, where she'd discovered the phone. Her gumption was at a level she'd never experienced before.

"What are you doing now?" Josh yelled after her impatiently.

"I'm going to call the car service and ask to be picked up," Carly responded trenchantly. "I assume you sleep at night same as everyone else."

Josh ground his jaw. She was getting real carried away now.

The phone was close enough to the opening into the living room for Josh to hear her end of the call. He was able to put together that there wasn't a driver available at the moment.

"I have to call back in an hour," Carly told him aloofly as she crossed in front of him and headed to the den. "I'm going to be looking at my uncle's papers."

Josh watched her close the door of the den behind her. He brought his hands to his head. If he hadn't had a headache before, he had one now. A tall, lanky, redheaded headache.

Chapter Three

Josh looked over at the den's closed door. Carly had been in there just about an hour now. He'd spent the time pacing around, turning the TV off and on and off again. He'd thought about going over to the bunkhouse to hang out. Considered getting on his bike and heading out for the night. Instead he'd downed a beer and stayed antsy.

Josh checked his watch again. Why wasn't she coming out to call the car service? Was she that engrossed in paperwork that she'd lost track of time? Oh, God, Josh groaned to himself. Was she in there crying?

With that last thought in mind, Josh vaulted up from the couch and walked to the den. He opened the door to see she was sitting at the desk, her face down on her arm, the back of her head to him. Her red hair was just barely under the control of the pins she used to keep it on the top of her head.

He was sure now she was crying—had undoubtedly been crying the whole time. With a deep breath, he shifted feet, leaning on first one hip then the other. He felt downright lousy that he'd brought her to tears.

"Carly..." he whispered.

When she didn't acknowledge him, he walked up to her. She wasn't crying. She was fast asleep. He heard the tiniest little snore as he took in what he could see of her face.

She'd put on glasses and they'd fallen to the tip of her nose. One side of the wire frame was held in place around the ear she had resting on her arm. The other side of the frame was caught in her hair, but awry at her cheek. From what he could tell, her closed eyes didn't seem to be puffy.

Josh looked away from her to draw in a large breath of relief. He noticed that she'd draped her green blazer over the head of the moose on the wall. She hadn't just duked it out with him. It looked as if she'd also battled the moose.

Still fast asleep, Carly shifted her face a little. Her eyeglasses lost their perch at the tip of her nose to dangle in front of her mouth. Josh watched as Carly wiggled her body, trying to make herself comfortable. He didn't see any sense to her going to a motel now. He could probably carry her into the bedroom without even waking her.

Josh rubbed his thumb back and forth across his lips. He thought about his earlier offer to lift her up in order to keep her shoes from getting all muddy—an

offer she'd immediately refused. Had she thought he
was making a pass at her? *Had* he been making a
pass? No way, was the instantaneous response Josh
gave himself.

Slowly, he reached out and removed her glasses. He
placed them on the desk on top of the scraps of paper
she'd sorted into piles. She didn't even stir. Bending
down, Josh took the hand that was hanging loose at
her side and carefully wrapped it around his neck.
Turning his body a little, Josh got her head to the
crook of his neck. He snaked one hand in just under
her shoulders, his other hand under her knees.
Counting to three, he rose with Carly in his arms.

Josh found himself totally aware of her body's
slender curves. He was even more aware that her
breasts were fuller than his eyes had observed in the
loose-fitting clothing she seemed to favor. He certainly wasn't trying to take advantage of her, but he
did have one hand where it shouldn't have been. He
would have had to shift her to move it.

He stood poised, waiting to see if she was going to
wake. All he heard was a little mew while her other
hand sinuously found its way around his neck to meet
the one he'd already placed there. Josh felt his body
tighten. She might not know how to be provocative
when she was awake, but she was doing a damn good
job of it in her sleep.

Josh walked slowly toward the bedroom, trying not
to jar her, while making a determined effort to keep his
hand from misbehaving more than it already was.
Through her shirt and bra Josh could tell that her

nipple had puckered up to his palm. It was discon-
certing the hell out of him.

He hit the light switch with his elbow as he stepped
with her into the bedroom where he'd placed her luggage earlier. Anxious to get her out of his arms, Josh
increased his stride as he walked to the double bed. As
he placed her on the made-up mattress, her hands
dropped from around his neck, then came up again to
wrap tenaciously around his back.

He heard her mew again, which was starting to
sound more like a moan. A sultry kind of moan.
Bracing his elbows on the bed, Josh took in a jerky
breath. He waited a moment, then put his palms to the
mattress, trying to extricate himself without waking
her. But as he raised himself some, he heard her moan
again. This one wasn't sultry. It was a complaint.

Josh studied her. He now found a few faint freckles across the bridge of her nose. They didn't lessen the
appeal of her face any.

Another little moan jerked Josh's gaze to her
mouth. She had a tiny beauty mark above one corner
of her upper lip, close enough to be covered if she was
being kissed the way she should be kissed. An agitated thought moseyed into Josh's head to accom-
pany his observation. Furious with himself, Josh
pushed it out, squashing a ludicrous impulse to find
out what it would feel like to kiss her. Was he losing it?

Carly stirred and made a protesting sound. Her
hands came down from around his back. Josh
straightened up and watched her curl herself into a
new position. Going to the closet, he pulled an extra
blanket down from the shelf. He carefully covered her

with it, then waited to hear if she was going to moan
again. She did, but it sounded contented this time and
was accompanied by a slight snore. Her snore nudged
a smile to Josh's lips. Switching off the lamp, he
walked out of the room.

His smile had disappeared by the time he walked
into the bunkhouse's mess hall, his toothbrush, shav-
ing gear and a change of clothes in hand.

"Hey, hey, hey." Paulie gave a foxy grin. "You get
yourself thrown out?" He was shuffling a deck of
cards. Ben and Billy Jack were with him at the table.

"No. It was my decision," Josh grunted, which was
as far as he cared to go with this topic. Tossing his be-
longings aside, he took a seat at the table. "Cut me
in," he said shortly.

"I've been thinking," Ben piped up. "I don't agree
that our bet should be off. She looks hot to me."

Josh felt himself tighten. "Is there a female that
doesn't look hot to you?"

"Not many." Ben smiled, not insulted.

"Did you guys have a bet about her?" Billy Jack
asked, getting into the discussion.

"Yeah," Ben answered. "What do you think, Billy
Jack? You've got the deciding vote."

"I liked her," the young man answered self-
consciously. "She seems really sweet."

Josh suddenly couldn't dislodge from his mind the
feel of Carly Gerard in his arms, her breast filling his
hand. He could still hear her sultry moan in his head.

Yanking some bills out of his pocket, Josh peeled
one off. "It's worth twenty to me for you to shut up."
He slapped the bill down in front of Ben.

"You can't say that I don't come cheap." Ben picked the twenty up from the table with aplomb and stuck it into his pocket.

"I still want to know how come you're here and she's there," Paulie needled.

"Are you going to deal or what?" Josh asked sharply.

"Get ready to lose," Paulie said with a grin, passing out the cards.

That wasn't a novel idea, Josh thought to himself. He'd already lost round one with Carly Gerard.

Carly opened her eyes and stretched. Raising her head a little, she looked about for a clock. She looked for a TV. Every motel room had a TV. It came to her with a jolt that she wasn't in a motel room. She was still in the cabin.

Carly sat up quickly. The blanket covering her fell down to her lap, revealing that she was still in her clothes. She was still in her clothes, and in a bedroom of the cabin of which half belonged to Josh Spencer.

Frazzled, Carly got out of bed. The door of the bedroom was open, allowing her to see into part of the living room. She walked to the door, but didn't see Josh Spencer around, though she did hear some noise coming from the kitchen.

"Did you sleep well?" Josh asked the minute he saw her. He'd checked on her when he'd come back to the cabin just minutes ago. She'd still been asleep, moaning a little, snoring a little. He'd left the door open to hear her get up.

"Fine," Carly answered, still feeling discombobulated. "How did I..."

"I carried you." Josh sent her a smile. He was determined to be pleasant. He wouldn't even have minded apologizing for the way their last conversation had gone. All he wanted to do was buy her out. Calmly, coolly and collectedly.

"You carried me?" Carly echoed, trying to conjure up the image in her mind. She'd never been carried by a man before. She wasn't the carried-by-a-man type. Was she supposed to say thank-you?

Josh nodded his head. He even extended her another smile. This one stayed on his mouth a little longer. He was taking in her hair, which was completely chaotic. A thick bright red spiraling wave lay across her forehead, almost blocking half her vision.

"In case you're wondering, I slept in the bunkhouse." He figured she'd want to know that.

She turned her head aside, hoping to break her fresh awareness of his sexual attractiveness. And he wasn't even wearing his Stetson. "Is it all right with you if I use the shower?" She was breathing in the heady scent of his after-shave, while at the same time trying to bring to the surface some thought running around in her head. She couldn't capture it, but her pulse had suddenly gone into overdrive.

"It's half yours," Josh quipped. "I'll get breakfast going. Do you like eggs?" He hadn't needed an alarm clock this morning. He hadn't slept much, though the bed in the bunkhouse had been more than comfortable. He'd lain awake for quite a while wondering if she'd woken after he'd left and called the car service

to take her to the motel. It wasn't an issue, or any kind
of point, but he'd spent some time on it. He'd spent
even more time feeling lousy about the way his buy-
out conversation had gone. He knew he'd hurt her
feelings.

"Thank you, but I don't want to put you out." The
thought that had been running around her head now
came to a stop. She remembered exactly where they
stood—and it wasn't on the same side. Her pulse was
still hammering. Confrontations of any kind was not
her forte.

Josh didn't care for the stony response she'd just
handed him. He was bending over backward to make
this easy on both of them. "Fine," he replied coolly,
getting the cool part of calm, cool and collected down
pat.

"If you don't mind, I will have some coffee after I
shower," she said, uncomfortable with the shift in his
disposition. *She* was trying to be businesslike and polite. Why couldn't he be the same?

Josh cocked his head. "Would you rather make
your own coffee or is it okay with you to drink from
the pot I was planning to make?"

Carly didn't think his sarcasm was called for. Not
gracing him with an answer—not that she had one to
give—she turned and walked out.

As soon as she stepped under the spray of the
shower Carly rethought the manner of her response to
him this morning and the manner of his response to
her. Now that she was contemplating, she realized that
he had seemed friendly at first. Certainly not con-
frontational. Somehow or other she'd brought that

on. If businesslike and polite wasn't the way to go with him, what was?

Hair dripping wet, Carly uncapped her bottle of shampoo. She washed her hair once. Conditioned it twice.

Finished with her hair, Carly reached for the bar of soap in the recessed shelf of the tiled wall.

His soap.

Soap that he used to lather his body.

Soap that he used to lather his *nude* body.

Exasperated with her imagination, Carly quickly lathered her skin. The temperature of the water was just right, but she had goose bumps all over.

Half an hour later, Josh looked up from the table as Carly came back into the kitchen. She was wearing a blue denim shirt, jeans and a pair of black leather boots. He realized they were dressed almost identically, though his denim shirt was a darker shade of blue and his jeans were better fitted to his hips and legs than hers were. Her thick curly hair was pulled back into a ponytail, looking for the most part blow-dried. The ends appeared to be still damp.

Carly picked up the mug he'd set out for her and poured herself a cup of coffee. She added milk and two heaping teaspoons of sugar.

Josh had already drunk two cups of coffee before he'd cooked a couple of eggs for himself. He was polishing off the first of his eggs as Carly took a seat opposite him at the table.

Carly looked sideways at him as she brought her coffee mug to her mouth. The egg he was eating was fried, the white all crisp, the yolk still soft. It was just the way she liked her eggs. He even dipped his toast into the yolk the way she did.

"My offer is still open," Josh said, catching her eyeing his plate as he forked the last of his second egg into his mouth. "How do you like your eggs?"

"The same as yours. Just one, though." Carly ventured a small smile, deciding this time to try to follow his lead. She'd never had a man cook her breakfast before. For that matter, she'd never had breakfast with a man, excluding her father, and her brother, who was three years older than she was.

"Why didn't you sleep in your room last night?" Carly asked as he took her egg from the refrigerator and cracked it into the frying pan he'd used for his.

Josh sent her a teasing look. There was a sheen to her freshly washed face. He spotted the few freckles she had, now that he knew exactly where to find them. "I thought you'd be uncomfortable about it."

He was right. That would have made her more uncomfortable than she already was. "Was it uncomfortable for you to bunk with the men? Being the boss and all?"

"I'm not that kind of boss." His blue eyes came back her way. "Is that the kind of boss you'd like to be?"

"No," Carly responded genuinely. She thought of her Hollywood idea of being a boss. It didn't fit her right anyway.

"What kind of boss did you have back in New York?" he asked, putting two slices of bread into the toaster for her.

"A dictator," Carly answered. "The Garment District is rampant with them."

Josh grinned. Carly gave him back a full smile.

"I guess you didn't like your job." He slid the cooked egg onto a plate and brought it over to the table with a clean fork, then went back for the toast.

"Actually, I did like my job. My immediate boss was great. The dictator's son. We got along just fine."

"How fine?" Josh gave her a rapscallion look as he took his seat at the table. He was curious about her personal life.

"Not that fine," she replied, liking her response.

Josh's mouth angled into another grin. "You did say that there was no guy back in New York?" He was keeping his repartee headed in the direction of his present interest. What kind of guy was she attracted to?

"No one in particular." This time Carly got it right, and she was even cutting into her egg at the same time. "Is there a woman in your life?" It wouldn't have surprised her any if he had to give out numbers.

"No one in particular," Josh responded lazily, watching the way she ate around the yolk, leaving it for last. It was the same way he ate his fried eggs.

"I would have thought that you had someone in your life." Carly said it without thinking whether she should or shouldn't as she broke the yolk and mopped it up with her toast.

"I would have thought you had someone in *your* life," Josh returned effortlessly. Was her naive sensuality a put-on? Or was it for real?

"There was someone a while ago." More than a year ago, to be exact. "He worked in the same building as I did. We met on the elevator." *We met on the elevator!* Why did you have to put that in? she asked herself.

"What happened?" Josh thought of the contours of her body, which he couldn't make out now with his eyes. Restlessly he tapped his fingers on the table.

"It didn't work out." Carly brought the dim impression of her relationship with Stan Reddings into focus. They'd ridden up and down the elevator together for a month before he'd even asked her out. The relationship had lasted eight months. It had been a nice, easy, steady relationship. A couple thing. Someone to be with. No fireworks, but that hadn't bothered her. She'd had one lover before Stan and there hadn't been any fireworks then either. As far as she was concerned, a match of personalities was the vital factor to a relationship. Everyone knew that passion didn't last.

"Not enough in common?" Josh broke into Carly's reverie.

She thought about how to answer. The truth was that Stan had met someone else. Someone in the same building. Someone who'd also ridden on the elevator while she'd been riding with him as a couple.

Carly nodded her head to Josh's suggested response. Thankfully, Stan Reddings had switched jobs a few weeks after breaking up with her. She'd been exhausted from ducking around corners and climbing ten flights of stairs in order to not run into him riding the elevator with someone else.

"What do you like to do for fun?" *Where are you heading with that question, Spencer? he asked himself. What* does that have to do with buying her out?

"For fun?" She liked to read. She loved movies. She enjoyed going to museums. Sometimes she knitted—not that she'd ever finished anything. God, she was dull!

"For fun," Josh repeated.

"The usual things," Carly answered finally. "Can I ask you something?"

"Okay."

"Why did you give up being a lawyer?" she asked, although she really wanted to know about his marriage. She was certain that the reason he didn't want a female partner had to do with his ex-wife.

"I didn't like the kind of person I was turning into. All I was thinking about was how much billing I could get into a day. I wasn't seeing people. I was only looking to take on as many clients as I could. Social occasions weren't even social occasions. They were just another way of drumming up business. A way to get ahead." Josh knew he would never let himself get caught up in that kind of money wheel again. He was happy with himself now, though every so often he did get a feeling that there was still something out of sync in his life.

Carly gave Josh an understanding look. "No time out to smell the roses?"

He winked. "Do roses grow in New York? I never saw any."

"You don't look like you'd be a lawyer." She'd never seen a lawyer as sexy as he was.

"What do I look like I'd be?"

Carly didn't hesitate. "You look like a cowboy."

Her answer surprised and delighted Josh.

"I look like what I am," Carly continued. "I look like a bookkeeper. I act like a bookkeeper. I fit the cliché."

"You don't fit any cliché. Not with that red hair of yours." Josh wanted to say more, but he didn't. It wasn't that he felt he'd be at any disadvantage by complimenting her. He just wanted to quit flirting with her.

Carly kept herself from inquiring just what he'd meant by that. She thought it might be sort of a compliment—not from the exact words as much as the way he'd said them. But she wasn't about to ask him. Excluding her father, she'd never had a man compliment her on her hair. Her red tresses drew comments, not compliments.

"Do you have plans for the day?" Carly asked instead.

"I'm pretty loose."

But Carly had a plan for herself. She planned to start learning everything she needed to show him that she would make him a good partner.

Josh watched Carly drink her cooled coffee. "Can I warm that up for you?"

"All right." Carly smiled her thanks.

Josh went over to the counter, came back with the coffeepot and he filled her mug. "About your staying in a motel... I don't see any sense to it. I can stay in the bunkhouse for now." He had blindsided her yesterday. He wanted to make up for it.

Carly dropped her gaze to the table. "I know you expect that I'm going to change my mind about all this."

"I'm not going to lie to you. I don't figure you to stay. I have an idea..." Josh paused because the idea was just coming to him.

"What idea?" Carly asked warily, looking at him directly now.

"How about I send a weekly check to you in New York? You can retain your share in the business. You wouldn't even have to go back to work."

"I like working," Carly answered tersely. She got up from the table, brought her dishes to the sink and began washing them as Josh watched.

Once she finished the task, Carly turned to face Josh. "I guess I'll see you later." Without waiting for any response, Carly headed out of the kitchen.

Her abrupt departure caught him unexpectedly. After a couple of seconds, Josh moved to the doorway leading out of the kitchen. He saw her heading for the front door. "Where are you going?"

"I'm going to find someone to teach me how to ride a horse," Carly threw back.

She didn't slam the door on her way out, but she might as well have. Her reply had that kind of effect on Josh. She was proving to be a tougher adversary than he'd envisioned.

Chapter Four

Josh waited impatiently for ten minutes before he left the cabin and sauntered to the back field. He tried to walk casually just in case she happened to look his way. Only she wasn't anywhere around. Josh spent the next ten minutes annoying himself by wondering whose offer she'd accept. Ben would be willing to teach her to ride, as would Paulie or even Billy Jack. Denny, if he was around, would have knocked the other three out of the running.

Why should he care who tried to teach her? he thought, running his fingers through his hair. He was letting himself miss the whole point here. The point was that his provoking her into feeling she needed to learn to ride hadn't sent her packing.

Just then Josh spotted Billy Jack leading a quiet chestnut filly named Lady Luck. Carly was with him, walking with her face turned toward the horse. Josh couldn't see her expression, but he was certain that it was somewhere between determined and scared to death.

"You did say this one is very gentle, right?" Carly said to Billy Jack. It was at her next heartbeat, which was speeding along, that Carly noticed Josh farther ahead. He wasn't looking her way, but was studying the wood fencing that ran the circumference of the pasture. He had a hammer in his hand.

"Miss Gerard, this filly is the gentlest animal I've ever seen," Billy Jack reassured her, coming to a halt midway into the pasture.

"Please call me Carly." She took a deep breath and tried to keep her concentration on Billy Jack. Josh's presence had her even more unnerved than she already was. The last person in the world that she wanted to make a fool of herself in front of was Josh Spencer.

"Carly." Billy Jack didn't make full eye contact, but he did give it a go.

"It is okay for me to call you Billy Jack, isn't it?" Carly asked distractedly, flipping a glance over at Josh. He was testing a post and rail by kicking at it with his Western boot.

"Well, sure. If you want to just call me Billy, that's okay, too."

Carly smiled and tried to relax. "I like Billy Jack. It sounds Western."

She noticed Billy Jack gave her a pleased look that was almost full-faced. She also took note that Josh had moved nearer to them, kicking posts on the way.

He had stuck some nails in his mouth that he'd pulled from his jeans pocket.

"Today you should just get used to the feel of sitting in a saddle," Billy Jack was saying. "Trotting around a little."

Carly thought that sounded like a snap. She smiled again and nodded her head.

"If you're ready, I'll show you how to mount."

Carly regarded Lady Luck. How did one get on top of a horse? She considered suggesting that they get a step stool.

"Just give me two minutes," she told Billy Jack. "Maybe I should limber up." Carly thought of the yoga classes she'd taken a few years back when it had been the fad to learn that kind of relaxation therapy. She'd managed to twist her body into all sorts of contortions. They weren't necessarily the ones being called for now, but they had to count for something.

"Take as long as you want," Billy Jack answered agreeably.

Josh watched from the sideline as Carly began some unusual body motions. She had her back to him, her ponytail swinging side to side. His eyes didn't remain on her blazing red hair long before dropping to her hips. She was doing something that could almost have been belly dancing. Josh's focus swung to Billy Jack, who was watching her with total fascination. What the hell was she doing?

Carly took in Billy Jack's bashful smile of encouragement. She pondered to herself that if she was looking for Mr. Right at the moment, Billy Jack would have been a perfect candidate. His personality was similar to hers, just like Stan Reddings's had been. Billy Jack was also nicer looking than Stan. Carly cogitated on her Mr. Right qualifications as she worked on her personally designed relaxation-exercise program. She was not letting herself think about Josh Spencer.

As limber as her unathletic body got, Carly breathed, "I'm ready," to Billy Jack. Not for anything was she going to glance Josh's way.

"Stand at Lady's side," Billy Jack instructed after using one hand to wipe a line of sweat off his brow. He had Lady's reins wrapped around his other hand.

Carly raised her eyes heavenward. *Please let me do this. Please...* Then she took a stance at Lady's side.

"You can stroke her if you like," Billy Jack suggested.

Carly gingerly put her hand to the horse. She lightly patted the animal, then took her hand off.

"Grab hold of the horn of the saddle."

Carly grabbed as tight a hold as she could, lacing her fingers together and hooking her thumbs. Her knuckles quickly turned white.

"Put your right foot in the stirrup."

"My right foot?" Carly rasped. It was her left foot that was closest to the stirrup at the side she was standing at.

"Let me demonstrate for you first," Billy Jack said, and came around to Carly.

Carly let go of the horn, took a giant step aside and gave Billy Jack her spot. She hadn't been breathing all that deeply, but enough to decide that she wasn't keen on Lady Luck's aroma.

Billy Jack mounted in slow motion, and Carly observed every one of his movements. It didn't look all that difficult.

With the same couple of nails still between his lips, Josh observed Carly watching Billy Jack. The hammer Josh was holding was raised, but forgotten. It didn't matter. The fence didn't need fixing. He'd just gone over it a few days ago.

Billy Jack dismounted with ease. "Okay. Now you try."

Carly grabbed the horn again in the same fashion as she had before. She put her right foot in the stirrup, and leaned forward the way Billy Jack seemed to have. Not breathing through her nose, Carly took in a mouthful of Lady Luck's mane.

"You're leaning forward too much." Billy Jack pointed out the obvious.

Carly sent Billy Jack a testy glance, which she immediately took back, offering a look of apology in its place while she spit some horsehairs out of her mouth. She was too overwhelmed with this daring adventure she'd brought on herself to even think about being ladylike.

"Put your foot back into the stirrup and put all your weight to your right side," Billy Jack began again. "Then bring your left leg up and swing it over the saddle. You can put your arms around Lady Luck's neck and try it that way."

Josh had moved even nearer now to Carly and Billy Jack. He could hear every word that was being said, even though the younger man was speaking in a low voice. Josh took the nails out of his mouth to groan under his breath. He could just see her falling off Lady Luck and breaking her neck. He wouldn't have minded wringing her neck for her obstinacy.

Carly decided she wasn't going to put her arms around Lady Luck's neck. She'd probably choke the poor animal. She tried the same movement she'd tried before, but not leaning quite as much forward. But her left leg still wasn't interested in going over. Carly was just about to throw in the towel when she spotted Josh. Their eyes met for a second before they both quickly broke off the glance. Carly made herself remember every single word of wild bravado she'd issued to him the night before. She wasn't going to back down. She was going to prove herself to him. Or kill herself trying. Whichever came first....

"If you wouldn't mind me putting my hands on you," Billy Jack said sheepishly, "I could give you a boost."

Carly looked at Billy Jack as if he were her savior. She wouldn't have minded taking a boost from the devil right now.

Billy Jack put his hands at Carly's waist. "Put your weight on me and try bringing your left leg up and over now."

Josh watched the scene unfolding in front of him and tensed. He didn't want to think about it, but the tension he was feeling was the kind a guy feels when another guy tries to make time with his woman. Josh negated that suggestion as quickly as it had come. Carly Gerard was not his woman! There wasn't any way that he wanted her to be his woman. *His woman!* When had he started thinking in cowboy lingo?

Josh had a full sense of where Billy Jack's hands were—not that they were all that near to where Josh's own hand had been when he'd carried Carly into the bedroom. But Billy Jack's hands were pretty close. Josh could clearly make out a flush of heat on the younger man's face. He didn't need a road map to figure out the direction that Billy Jack's mind was taking as he moved Carly closer to himself with one hand while he used his other hand to raise her left thigh.

Carly didn't know exactly how it happened, but the next thing she knew she was seated in the saddle. An exultant smile came across her mouth—one she shared with Billy Jack. Surreptitiously Carly looked for Josh. She didn't glance his way for long—just long enough to pick up his frown. For a second, Carly thought about making a face at him.

"How do you feel?" Billy Jack asked, drawing Carly's eyes fully his way.

"High up," she answered nervously, and got another smile from Billy Jack.

Josh pulled his gaze from Carly to Billy Jack before positioning a nail against one of the fence posts. He hammered it in so hard he nearly split the wood. Josh knew exactly why Billy Jack was smiling.

"I'm going to walk Lady around a little. Ready?" Billy Jack asked.

"Ready," Carly murmured, making herself breathe in and out. She even endeavored to do it with her mouth closed.

The reins in his hand, his gaze fixed on Carly, Billy Jack walked the filly around. Once again Carly's eyes

met Josh's, but the visual linkage was broken as Billy
Jack turned Lady Luck. Josh was left with the sight of
Carly's back and the filly's rump.

"How are you doing?" Billy Jack asked.

"Fine. I think." Carly spoke carefully. Her hips
were swaying, but she was still balanced and Lady
Luck was moving underneath her.

"I'm just going to pick up Lady's trot a little.
Okay?"

Carly exhaled a deep breath she hadn't realized
she'd been holding in and bobbed her head in agreement.

Josh banged another nail into the same post. This
time he did split the wood and had to hit nails on either side to hold the crack together. By then he was
able to see Carly's face again. She was sitting the saddle rod-stiff, but there was a satisfied glint in those
large hazel eyes. What really kicked him in the rear
was the admiration he was feeling at the way she was
hanging in.

With just the slightest twist of her head, not wanting to chance shifting her posture any, Carly darted a
look over to Josh. She wanted him to be impressed.

Josh looked away, not wanting her to see that she
had his attention. He hit another nail, banged his finger and cursed under his breath.

"Would you like to try holding the reins?" Billy
Jack asked, looking at Carly with obvious admiration.

Say no, Josh wanted to scream. Unconsciously he
shook his head while he sucked on his throbbing finger. He didn't think she was ready yet.

"I guess I could try it," Carly answered, holding herself in tight anticipation. She'd never been daring. But this was the new Carly Gerard.

Billy Jack held Lady steady while he offered the reins to Carly.

Unlocking her grasp of the saddle's horn as she reached out, Carly teetered a bit. For one long moment, Carly, Billy Jack and Josh all held their breath. Quickly, she grabbed the horn again. "I don't think I'm ready for the reins yet," came Carly's tremulous voice as her mind plummeted back to reality.

Josh threw a glare at Billy Jack for having stupidly suggested that she take the reins. But the young man didn't catch the look—his eyes were trained on Carly. He appeared totally smitten with her.

An hour later, still in the same stiff position she'd started in, Carly decided she'd done as much as her body was willing to allow for her first lesson. She had pins and needles in her legs, and her back and shoulder blades were aching.

Billy Jack brought Lady Luck to a halt. Then he verbally directed Carly on the dismounting procedure. "Kick your feet out of the stirrups. Bring your left leg over. Sit sideways in the saddle. I'll bring you down."

Carly couldn't move. She wanted to move. She just couldn't. She felt as far off the ground as if she were on top of the Empire State Building. Mounting Lady Luck had been hard enough. Dismounting seemed even more difficult. Would Lady Luck know not to rear or something like that?

Josh envisioned Billy Jack assisting Carly off the horse. He'd slide her down against his body. He wouldn't have told her to sit sideways if that wasn't what he had in mind. Sideways was not the way to dismount.

Josh tossed his hammer to the ground, spit out the nails he had between his lips and walked over to Billy Jack. "I'll take over from here. There's a corner of the billboard out front that looks like it's peeling. Check it out for me."

Billy Jack started to say something, then didn't. Not looking happy at being dismissed, he took off.

Carly was already embarrassed enough. She didn't need Josh Spencer adding to it by getting right up in her face. "Billy Jack was giving me a lesson," Carly said angrily.

"Billy Jack was finished," Josh replied nonchalantly. "I'll take you off the horse."

"I'll get down when I'm ready. I don't need your help," Carly countered mulishly.

Josh crossed his arms in front of his chest. One corner of his mouth hiked up in a grin. "You don't mind if I watch, do you?"

Carly uttered a string of expletives in her head—words she never used even under her breath. She was completely panicked. There wasn't any way she was going to be able to get off Lady Luck without someone assisting her.

"It's getting hot out." He teased her with his eyes.

Carly blinked at the moisture running down from her forehead. Frustrated, she kicked her feet free of the stirrups and then just sat that way. She told herself to rescind her refusal to accept his help, but stubbornness won out. *Don't move, Lady Luck. Please.* Carly prayed there was such a thing as telepathy and that it worked between humans and animals.

Josh's eyes came up from Carly's feet to check her expression. She still looked angry. "I'm going to put my hands on your waist." Not giving her any preparation time, he grasped her around her midsection.

Hot, bothered and flustered, Carly felt her cheeks grow redder than they already were. In order to do anything about Josh's hands, she would have had to remove her own from their grip on the saddle horn. And she was holding on to that horn for dear life.

Josh kept his blue eyes turned up to Carly's face. "Put your hands on my shoulders."

She gave her situation some additional thought—realistically, logically. Only her mind kept centering on the feel of his possessive hands at her waist and the chill going down her back. It wasn't the kind of chill that cooled her off any.

"Don't worry." Josh winked at her. "I've got you."

Carly made an attempt at giving him a mean look, which only made Josh grin. He would have yanked her off, but he was worried she'd work against him and hurt herself in the process.

"Don't make fun of me." She turned her head.

Josh's heart gave a thud. "I'm not making fun of you, Carly. Honest." Trying to soothe her, he moved his hands coaxingly up a little then back down to where they'd been.

Carly brought one of her hands up to dig into his shoulder, if for no other reason than to stop the movement of his hands. Her other hand followed a split second later.

Josh smiled encouragingly at her. "Now bring your left leg over the saddle and sit sideways."

Carly didn't realize how that positioning would place her until she did so and found Josh sandwiched between her thighs. Carly's cheeks turned even brighter than her hair.

Josh waited, wanting to give her time to regain her composure. He knew he shouldn't be doing what Billy Jack had planned. Then again, he was more of a cowboy in that arena than Billy Jack.

Stepping back, he drew Carly slowly down the front of his body until she had her feet to the ground. But he didn't let go of her. It wasn't that he was intentionally flirting with her now, he could just feel how shaky she was.

Carly finally pushed her palms to his chest and Josh dropped his hands. He did manage to hold her gaze before she turned. He wanted to tell her again that he hadn't been making fun of her, but before he was able to come up with the right words, she turned away.

Josh watched her retreat. She was walking bowlegged, with one hand at the base of her spine. He knew how much her body had to be hurting, and he knew how upset she was. Josh took a quicker route to the cabin than the one she was taking.

Carly heard the water running in the bathroom as she walked into the living room. There wasn't a single part of her body that wasn't in torture from her ride atop Lady Luck.

Looking over at the bathroom, she saw that the door was open. She made her way slowly to the doorway, only to find Josh waiting inside.

"The best thing right now is a long soak in a hot tub," he told her, pointing to the bathwater he was running.

"I don't need you taking care of me," Carly replied tersely. Embarrassment still had the better of her, though a good long soak did sound perfect.

Josh was becoming vexed by her determined willfulness. "Who do you want taking care of you? Billy Jack? You've got the poor guy shaking in his boots already."

"What does that mean?" Carly took up the best defensive stance she could. Not a muscle in her body was interested in complying.

"Don't you know when a guy is attracted to you?"

"He is not attracted to me," Carly replied indignantly.

"Yes, he is." Josh wondered if perhaps she hadn't realized it. "Are you attracted to him?"

"I'm not going to answer that." Carly thought about what Josh had said. She didn't feel physically attracted to Billy Jack, but now that she considered it, she did like the idea of having Josh Spencer think that Billy Jack was attracted to *her*. She liked that idea a lot.

"Billy Jack isn't all that experienced with women." Josh threw the information out, though he didn't know what point he was trying to make.

"I'm sure *you* are," Carly retorted, surprised at how quickly the remark flew from her mouth.

"If you need help getting undressed, I'm pretty good at that," Josh quipped, giving her the response she was asking for.

In your dreams, Carly was about to say, which was a phrase she'd heard used and played up for all it was worth. She'd never thought she'd get a chance to use it. Before she had the chance to try it out, Josh had exited the bathroom, closing the door behind him.

"In your dreams" would have been a stupid thing to say anyway, Carly chastised herself, getting undressed and stepping into the tub. Like she'd really be in his dreams!

Chapter Five

Carly came out of the bathroom a half hour later, clad only in a towel. She jumped when she saw that Josh was still in the cabin. She'd expected he'd gone back to fixing the fence, but here he was, looking at her near naked body. She had planned on putting her clothes back on after her long soak, then decided if she had to go through such agony and pain, she'd be better off changing into fresh clothing.

Josh was just as rattled seeing Carly in that towel, but he wasn't letting it show. It did take some doing to pull it off. He couldn't get his eyes off her legs. She had legs that didn't quit.

"I . . . didn't . . . think you were here," Carly spoke haltingly, totally discomposed.

Josh cleared his throat. "I figured you could use a massage." When the thought had come to him, it had seemed innocent. It didn't seem so innocent now. If he was looking for more trouble, he'd just picked a damn good way to find it.

"You mean you..." Carly gestured with her hand. Her clothes lay over her arm but as she moved, her bra dropped to the floor.

Josh took a few long steps and bent down to pick it up. Carly, also in the process of trying to bend, touched heads with him. It was more a brush of faces than a bang. Of course, it didn't take much of anything for Carly to feel even more awkward than she already was, standing in front of him for all intents and purposes practically nude.

"Did I hurt you?" He straightened up before she did. Her delicate white lace bra was dangling in his hand.

"No." Carly shook her head.

Josh took a look at her bra. He didn't get a chance to even think to gauge its size before she yanked it away from him.

Carly's face was all red again. She was trying to keep all of her clothes from falling while at the same time pressing one hand to where she had the towel secured above her breasts.

"Why don't you put some clothes on and I'll work those knots out of your back." Josh kept his eyes on her face, though that wasn't where his eyes wanted to be.

"I do appreciate your offer, but...ah..." She took some small steps to the side. "No massage." And with that, she fled to the bedroom and closed the door behind her.

Her pulse going crazy, Carly dug into her suitcase which she'd opened on the bed earlier. Screwing up her face in pain, she put on panties, another pair of loose jeans, and tried to fasten the hook of a bra. She gave up that idea after stifling a yelp. She settled instead for just putting on another denim shirt, not bothering to tuck it into her jeans. Her hair was half-wet and still somewhat caught in a ponytail. She didn't make any attempt to deal with it.

Carly came out of the bedroom barefoot, her breathing still rushed. She was fairly certain that Josh was still there.

She found him reclining on the couch, hands behind his head. He sat up as soon as he saw her.

"Don't you have something to do?" Carly asked nervously. She wasn't able to stop thinking about the massage he'd offered to give her. She knew what it felt like to have his hands on her. She got chills just thinking about it.

"No." Josh shrugged casually, but it was a put-on. He wasn't at ease. He was keyed up.

Carly considered going outside to sit on the porch stairs. She needed a lot of air. "How about the fence? Doesn't it need more fixing?" she asked, moving about the room.

"I was just pretending it needed fixing."

Carly stopped moving, her gaze widening on his face. "Why were you doing that?"

Josh pushed his fingers through his hair. "I didn't want to make you uneasy knowing that I was watching."

"Why were you watching?" Carly asked, not that she didn't know the answer. He'd obviously been looking to amuse himself.

Josh stuck his hand through his hair again. If he had any sense he'd just go and let her walk around in pain all day. "I wasn't going to leave you on your own to fall off and hurt yourself."

"I wasn't on my own. Billy Jack was with me." Had he really been worried about her? Carly sincerely doubted that.

"Billy Jack had enough to do to take care of Lady Luck. Horses don't always take well to novices." Josh didn't have any more answers. He didn't know why he'd gone out to watch her. He just had.

"I guess I should thank you." Carly wished she could understand what made him tick. He was a total enigma to her.

"You don't have to thank me," he said, getting to his feet. "Come here and lie down on the couch so I can give you a massage. There's no reason for you to stay in pain."

"I'm not in pain." Carly gave him a fib of rather tremendous proportion. "The bath did the trick. My body is totally relaxed now."

Josh grinned. "I'm not going to do anything that will compromise you." He thought of the trouble he would have been in if she hadn't put her clothes on. He wasn't positive he was immune even now. The image of her in just that towel wouldn't leave his head.

"I know you're not going to do anything that would compromise me. I wasn't thinking that. That would be the last thing I'd be thinking."

"Stop being skittish then," Josh said, coming up to her.

Carly's heart was racing. "I'm not being skittish. I just don't happen to need a massage."

"Prove it," Josh challenged.

"How?"

"Bend over and touch your knees."

"No," Carly answered resolutely. He couldn't make her.

"How about doing some of those moves you were doing before you got up on Lady Luck?" Josh thought about the expression on Billy Jack's face as he'd watched her get ready to mount the horse. "What were you doing those motions for anyway?"

"I was limbering up," Carly explained. His eyes were holding hers and she couldn't seem to pull her gaze away.

"Carly." Josh smiled. "Even Lady Luck gets a rubdown after a workout."

She took in a startled breath. "Are you suggesting that I should be treated like a horse?"

Josh groaned to himself. "What I'm saying is that you're going to be stiff as a board by tomorrow if you don't let me work those knots out of your back."

"I don't have any knots in my back," Carly stated adamantly.

"You're not a very good liar." He put his hands on her upper arms and gave her a light squeeze.

Carly winced.

"Now do you want to tell me again that you don't have any knots in your back?"

Her annoyed hazel eyes met the teasing light of Josh's blue gaze. "All right," Carly conceded, trying to sound indifferent. "If you want to give me a massage, give me a massage."

He pointed to the couch. "You're going to have to lay down."

Trying to act blasé, Carly went over to the couch and lay down with her back to him. She felt all jangled and gauche. Why couldn't she have been in the right line when blithesomeness and sophistication had been given out?

Josh put his knees to the floor as Carly turned her head to face the back of the couch. He moved her ponytail aside, but not before lightly letting the wet strands play against his hand.

Carly felt his fingers on her neck, palms to her shoulders, thumbs spread, taking position. Her arms were down at each side of her body, hands clenched into fists. But when his thigh brushed against the configuration of her hand, she quickly pulled that fist beneath her hip.

The tips of Josh's fingers began to move along the nape of her neck. The small tender rotations robbed Carly of what was left of her breath.

"You're even tighter than I thought."

Outwardly Carly did all she could to try and lie limp, passive and calm, but her highly erratic heartbeat contradicted her form.

Josh put his palms to work, pressing firmly against the knots in her shoulders. As unsettled as she was by his touch, her muscles were responding with palpable relief.

Josh's hands headed down to the middle of her back. "You're not wearing a bra," he said, caught by surprise at the discovery.

"I couldn't..." Carly's face burned with embarrassment, matching the heat of sensuality in her body that her mind hadn't been able to control. "Maybe I could try to put one on now."

"No," Josh answered thickly. "It's better this way."

Only it wasn't better for either Carly or Josh. His mind was resurrecting the feel of her breast nicely filling his hand just the night before and the way her nipple had hardened against his palm. And though Carly had no knowledge of where his hand had once been, it didn't stop her imagination from running amok. She gulped, doing all she could to keep the involuntary sound quiet.

Josh didn't have to worry about his fingertips accidentally straying this time. She had her arms glued to her sides, prohibiting him any access. His eyes slid down to the back of her knees and up again before doing a second take over her raised bottom.

He adjusted his libido and concentrated his gaze across the room while his hands roved. He wasn't going to touch her where he was thinking she probably needed to be touched the most.

Carly swiftly flipped over when Josh's fingers reached the base of her spine, just as his palms pushed against a very yielding part of her anatomy. She bolted up to a sitting position.

Josh reared back. "What?"

"You know what!" Carly was one big mass of frustration.

"Oh," Josh said, amusement clear in his voice. "I wasn't doing anything."

Carly gritted her teeth. She wished she'd affected him even a quarter as much as he'd been affecting her. It just wasn't fair.

"I wasn't going any lower." Josh looked at her gamely.

Carly slapped his face, without giving it any thought at all. She was shocked. She'd never slapped a man before.

Josh grabbed hold of both Carly's hands with just one of his. The slap she'd given him hadn't even left a sting. "If you slap a guy for doing nothing, he starts to think he should do something to deserve it." He wasn't ticked off that she'd slapped him. Actually, he'd thought it was kind of cute.

Carly looked wide-eyed at Josh.

Josh eyed her back. *Don't do it, Spencer!*

She had some sense of what he was about to do, but by the time his free hand came up to cradle the back of her head and his mouth covered hers, she'd lost all reason.

Carly couldn't hold her responsiveness back. She didn't even try. She just gave herself over to his lead. Her lips moved the way of his mouth, slowly and rhythmically. Her head lolled against the palm of his hand. She drifted along, dissolved into mindless pleasure.

He'd given more than one thought to her mouth, enough to know exactly how he wanted to treat it. But in that moment of first contact, Josh could only remember that whatever it was he'd considered doing, he didn't want to do it in a rush.

He kissed her inquisitively, exploring his way. Her mouth remained closed for the most part, but her lips were warm, pliable and very compelling. Josh could feel himself wanting to put his hands on her unguarded breasts, which were enticingly near his chest.

Carly suddenly realized that at some point—some totally uninhibited point—she'd locked her arms around his neck. She hadn't been aware of him even letting go of his hold on her hands. She probably wouldn't have comprehended it now except for the shock of fireworks going off inside her head at the first wet stroke of his tongue inside her mouth. His forearm held her securely about the waist, pressing her so close that she was hardly sitting on the couch any longer. He'd moved her to where she was straddling his hips.

Josh felt her lips go still. Mouths still connected, Carly took her hands down from his neck. Josh removed his arm from around her waist and their lips separated.

Jerkily, Carly pushed back into the cushion of the couch. She was breathless. She didn't think her heart was ever going to calm down. The embarrassment she'd experienced riding Lady Luck didn't begin to compare with the embarrassment she was feeling now. She wanted to get up from the couch, but she couldn't. He was in her way.

Josh got to his feet after a much needed cool-down pause. He couldn't believe he'd let himself get so involved. "I'm sorry. That was really stupid," he said.

"Exactly," Carly uttered. Whatever verbal skills she had were not at her disposal at the moment.

Josh ran his hand through his blondish-brown hair. "Let's just forget it."

"Exactly." Had she really felt fireworks? Was that what all the talk about passion was about?

"We seem to have gotten ourselves into a battle of the sexes."

Whatever you do, Carly, don't say "exactly" again.

"Exactly." Carly added a nod of her head this time. Her eyes were fixed on his flat abdomen. She didn't want to look higher or lower.

Josh pushed his hands into the pockets of his jeans. "Maybe it's more a battle of wills." *Stop talking this thing to death, Spencer. You kissed her. It was stupid. Just drop it.*

"A battle of wills?" Carly managed to string four whole words together into an unnecessary question.

Before he could explain his meaning, there was a knock on the outside door.

"Come in," Josh yelled.

The door opened and a man, whom Carly had never seen before, entered. He was middle-aged, bald and heavyset. He wore a short-sleeved white shirt, navy slacks, thick glasses, and carried a briefcase in one hand.

"Hi, Jimmy," Josh acknowledged. "I forgot you were coming out today." Bringing his eyes back to Carly, Josh said, "This is Jimmy Blatts. The accountant."

Doing all she could to pull herself together, Carly got to her feet and shook hands with Jimmy Blatts.

She didn't think she looked as if she'd just been kissed. She hadn't been wearing lipstick, so there were no smears to worry about. But her face felt hot.

"I'm glad to meet you," Jimmy said with a smile.

Carly's mouth was dry, but she did get herself to offer a mannerly response. "I'm glad to meet you, too."

"I guess we should go into the den," Josh injected. He wasn't in the mood for a meeting right now, but he was relieved to break off the conversation he'd just been having with Carly.

The three walked into the den and Jimmy took the seat behind the desk. Josh pulled up two chairs to the front of the desk and waited for Carly to sit before taking the chair next to her.

Jimmy Blatts retrieved some papers from his brief-case and laid them on top of the desk. "I guess you've had a chance to look around," he said to Carly.

"Some," she answered, covertly glancing at Josh.

The accountant handed Carly a profit-and-loss statement. She stared at the figures without really making much out. Nor was she paying much attention to the steady stream of words Mr. Blatts was speaking regarding the business.

Carly *was* aware of every time Josh ran his fingers through his hair. Five times so far. He'd rubbed the back of his neck twice.

Josh finally cut into Jimmy's monologue. "Carly is a bookkeeper. If you leave us all the statements, I'm sure she'll be able to go through them for herself. She can call you if she has any questions."

"A bookkeeper. That's great," Jimmy said. "If you want to keep the set of books that I've got going and bring me in once or twice a year instead of monthly, you'll be saving the business that expense."

Carly brightened. That was certainly one way she could be valuable as a partner. "I'm sure I could take over the books."

"I'll bring everything out by the end of the week and I'll help you get started." Jimmy Blatts took a few more papers out of his briefcase, placed them on the desk, then got to his feet.

Carly and Josh pushed back their chairs and stood.

"I'll see myself out," the accountant said, heading for the doorway.

Carly held herself tense, waiting for Josh to say something once it was just the two of them in the room. Her gaze flitted around a bit before noticing that something in the room had changed. The mounted moose head was gone.

Carly looked sideways at Josh. "What happened to the moose?"

"I took it down while you were soaking in the tub, and brought it to the bunkhouse." Josh had decided to stop being annoyed with his earlier actions. He'd kissed her. She'd kissed him back. He was a man. She was a woman. It had just been one of those momentary things. Not something to make a big deal about.

"Oh," Carly said.

Josh gave Carly a knowing wink. "I hung up your jacket in the hall closet."

His teasing gave Carly license to smile. She'd forgotten she'd thrown her jacket over the stuffed head.

"I gather you didn't like your uncle's moose," Josh ribbed.

Still smiling, Carly slowly shook her head. "Did you?"

"Not particularly." Josh grinned. "Gabby took it for his room. The guys thought it might look good hanging in the mess hall, but I vetoed them."

Carly took in the continued tease in his eyes. She knew he wasn't making fun of her. What he was doing was having fun with her. "I'm glad it won't be hanging in the mess hall. I wouldn't be able to eat again," she said, echoing his repartee.

"Speaking of eating," Josh said loosely, "I'm starving. How about you?" Now this was normal behavior, Josh decided, congratulating himself.

"Famished." Carly surprised herself at the ease with which she'd affected a light, almost breezy tone.

"I usually have lunch here in the cabin on Mondays and Tuesdays. Gabby just does dinner on days we're not putting on a show. There's cold cuts and cheese in the refrigerator. There might be some tuna around."

"What are you having?" Carly asked as they walked side by side out of the den and into the living room.

"Turkey, ham and swiss."

"All together?" Carly tilted her face toward him. It seemed to her that he'd forgotten all about having kissed her. Of course, she reminded herself, he *had* said he was going to forget it. *Couldn't he have kept it in his head for a little while?*

"All together. Mustard on one side and mayo on the other."

"I've never known anyone to put mustard and mayo together." Carly rolled her eyes.

Once in the kitchen, Josh went to the refrigerator. "Just for that, I'm going to make you taste my sandwich."

Carly teased back, "I'll make it for you since you made breakfast, but I refuse to taste it."

"Oh, yeah," Josh threatened teasingly.

"Yeah," Carly countered challengingly.

He threw her a grin as he opened the refrigerator. "Am I the first guy you've ever slapped?"

Carly flushed instantly, but it didn't stop her from lying. "No. It's happened before."

Josh arched his brow.

Carly read the look. "I didn't do it right, is that it?"

"Next time you have to do it to a guy, put more oomph into it." Josh winked, then hoped he hadn't changed the mood any. He was hoping to continue kidding around with her.

Now that the subject was back out, neither Carly nor Josh could get the kiss between them out of their minds. They both made themselves active. Josh took the tinfoil-covered cold cuts and cheese out of the refrigerator and put them on the counter. Carly began unwrapping them. Josh went for the bread, then the mustard and mayo. He put a knife and two plates on the counter.

"Not on the same piece of bread." Josh stopped Carly from spreading mayo on top of mustard. "Put the ham and swiss down on the mustard. Put the turkey over the swiss, then mayo on the other slice of bread.''

"That sounds better," Carly said, following his instructions, hoping he'd move away. He was standing practically on top of her, one elbow braced on the counter. She wished she hadn't responded to him the way she had when he'd kissed her. *He'd* just been making a point. *She* didn't have any excuse for her embarrassing behavior.

Josh thought to himself that he'd never met anyone like her. Shy and vulnerable one minute, looking to go nose to nose with him the next. Downright provocative when she was being kissed. "Are you willing to try my combo now?"

He was teasing her again. Carly set an impish smile on her mouth. "It really does look good. I'm going to make the same for myself." Carly put the sandwich she'd made on a plate and handed it over to him.

Josh took it to the table and sat down.

"What would you like to drink with it?" Carly asked, before beginning to prepare a sandwich for herself.

"There's beer in the refrigerator. Do you drink beer?"

"Sure," Carly answered, going to the refrigerator and taking out two bottles. She drank wine occasionally. But she did not like beer.

"I don't need a glass, but there are some in the cabinet to the right of the sink," Josh told her. He hadn't started eating his sandwich, as he was waiting for her to join him.

Since she was now trying on a new persona, Carly decided not to bother with a glass for herself. "I think the only way to drink beer is out of the bottle. Or the can." She brought the bottles of beer to the table and put them down.

Josh grinned as he twisted off both caps. "Somehow I don't picture you drinking beer from a bottle or can. I see you more with a glass of wine." He was recalling the wine stain she'd had on her skirt when he'd picked her up at the airport. He remembered how she'd looked in the boxy suit she'd been wearing yesterday. He wondered why she didn't show off her slim shape. Carly Gerard was not an easy woman to figure out.

"You should never try to judge a book by its cover," Carly bantered as she put her sandwich together, making her own a lot less thick than the one she'd made for him.

Josh slid one of the bottles of beer over to Carly as she took a seat at the table. "Cheers." He raised his bottle and took a deep swallow.

"Cheers." Carly raised her own bottle and took a small sip. Beer still didn't appeal to her palate.

Josh eyed her as she put the bottle down and picked up half of her sandwich. Her ponytail had fully dried into riotous curls and waves. He thought about the remark she'd made about not judging a book by its cover.

"It was very nice of Jimmy Blatts to suggest saving the business accounting costs," Carly said, after she'd finished chewing.

"Uh-huh," Josh replied, taking another large swallow of beer from his bottle. He didn't want to get into a business discussion with her right now. He picked up half of his sandwich and took the size of two bites to her one. "How's the sandwich?"

"Good." Carly smiled. "You know what I think? I think what this business needs most is some strong advertising." She hadn't looked very closely at the statements that the accountant had laid out, but she had noticed that there wasn't much money being spent on promotion.

Josh took another swig of his beer, then picked up his sandwich again. He devoured one half and picked up the second half. He didn't say anything.

Carly went on, putting her serious mind into action. "I know advertising on TV has to be very expensive, but maybe we could try it for a short period of time and see what happens. Have you ever tried any TV ads?"

Josh shook his head. He finished his sandwich and went back to his beer.

"How about newspaper ads outside of Oklahoma? I'm sure you run ads in Oklahoma." Carly was so involved in trying to be brilliant, she was totally unaware of Josh's growing irritation. "There's lots of land here not being fully utilized. If we can bring in more people we can enlarge the setup...put in more seating...a souvenir shop. Definitely a souvenir shop. We could even add a motel and a restaurant. Of course, not right away...."

"Carly." Josh said her name so brusquely that she blinked.

"Yes." Carly put herself on alert.

"I'm perfectly happy with the way the business is. We're turning a profit. It's paying out decent wages and no one is complaining. We have flyers out at tourist stops throughout Oklahoma, Texas, New Mexico and Arizona. A lot of people cross the country by car and we're on a fairly well-traveled road. We pull in enough business." Women were all the same, Josh reminded himself. They didn't think without seeing dollar signs in their heads.

Carly refused to have him see how upset he'd just made her by dismissing her the way he had. "I realize that I might be premature by making any suggestions. I haven't even gotten my feet wet yet. I know you're concerned about having a new partner. Personally I don't feel partners have to think alike on every issue. Did you and my uncle agree on everything?"

"As a matter of fact, we did." Josh gripped his bottle of beer tightly in his hand.

"Everything?" Carly was at a loss.

"The bottom line, Carly, is that I'm not interested in changing anything about this business. Why don't you just let me buy you out? I'm sure you can find any number of small businesses that would be interested in expanding."

"I'm not interested in selling my share in this one," Carly replied firmly, using every ounce of recently uncovered gumption she had in her system. This was her inheritance. Her uncle had meant for her to have it. No other business would mean the same to her. She could be an asset as a partner. She was sure of it.

"Well." Josh got to his feet. He couldn't see that there was anything more to say right now. He wasn't stymied. Eventually, she was going to get tired of butting heads with him.

Carly would have tried to come up with something more to say, but she didn't get to offer any other reasoning to justify her position. He walked out of the kitchen and out of the cabin, leaving her with half a sandwich to finish and a bottle of beer.

Chapter Six

"I'll go get Carly," Billy Jack offered buoyantly.

All the men were at the table in the mess hall. Gabby was putting the finishing touches to the dinner he'd prepared.

Josh had been just about to get up and get her himself, but Billy Jack was already heading for the door faster than Josh had ever seen him move.

Paulie grinned. "Billy Jack's been like a bull in a china shop all day. He's got a case for her. A megacase."

"Yeah," Josh said shortly. "I've noticed."

"I've got to say she has a way about her that could get a guy thinking about settling down if he had a yen for settling down," Ben put in.

"Don't any of you lug nuts go taking advantage of

her," Gabby called over. "I'm setting to have a nice long talk with Billy Jack."

"Give me a break, Gabby," Ben countered. "I'm talking nice."

"I heard you," Gabby retorted. "You just keep in mind that she's not your type."

"She's female, ain't she?" Ben pestered Gabby.

Gabby raised a ladle threateningly in the air.

Paulie grinned and turned to Josh. "Think she'd go for Billy Jack?"

"How should I know?" Josh's tone was lethally abrupt.

Paulie sent a look to Ben, then looked back again at Josh. "We know what's got you by the horns, but don't take it out on the rest of us."

"*What's* got you by the horns?" Gabby asked, placing a large tureen of piping-hot chili on the table.

Josh kicked back in his chair, trying to loosen himself up. "Nothing's got me by the horns."

"It's just his time of the month," Ben said humorously.

Josh feigned a grin and took the ribbing.

The first thing Carly saw as she entered the mess hall with Billy Jack was the smile on Josh's face.

"Did you finish checking out the statements?" he asked her, his smile fading. He figured that was what she'd been doing all afternoon, as he hadn't seen her anywhere around the grounds. She was wearing the same clothes she'd had on when he'd given her a massage, except that her denim shirt was now tucked into her jeans. She'd redone her hair, and it was now neatly twirled on top of her head. He figured she'd put her bra back on, too. He had to stop himself from undressing her in his mind. At least down to just a towel.

"I finished looking at them, and I called Jimmy Blatts to go over a few things," Carly replied aloofly while Billy Jack pulled out a chair for her.

Josh nodded his head indifferently.

This time Carly sat opposite Josh, and next to Billy Jack.

"Didn't know if you liked chili, little gal," Gabby said, bringing over a platter with thick slices of homemade bread. "I made you a couple of lamb chops just in case."

Carly smiled, overwhelmed and touched by Gabby's attention. "Please don't make extra work for yourself on my account. Whatever you're cooking is fine for me."

Josh took in the way Gabby was fussing over her like a mother hen. He could just imagine the conversation Gabby would be looking to have with him if the older man knew he was determined to push her out of the business.

Carly wondered if Gabby would take offense if she offered to help out in the kitchen. She wasn't particularly proficient at cooking, but she could chop things, bread things, and she could certainly clean up.

"You taste the chili if you like, little gal, but lamb chops are better for you." Gabby walked back to the stove.

Carly knew that Josh had his eyes in her direction, which was why she turned not only her face, but her shoulder toward Billy Jack. "I didn't get a chance to thank you for the riding lesson today."

"You did good. Real good," Billy Jack replied, gazing at her.

"I didn't do all that well," Carly answered self-consciously.

"Billy Jack told me that you did good. Really. I wouldn't say it now if Billy Jack hadn't said so," Paulie put in eloquently. "It isn't easy to learn how to ride."

Ben added a boost. "I don't know how I'd do if I had to learn now. We all learned to ride before we could walk. It's much harder to learn as an adult."

Carly gave Billy Jack, Ben and Paulie a smile of gratitude for lifting her spirits.

Josh was helping himself to some chili as Carly's eyes came his way. He hadn't failed to notice that smile of hers that she'd given the other men. He felt like the odd man out.

Carly thought about the battle of the sexes she was waging with Josh Spencer. Though she'd never seen him on a horse, she was certain he rode well. Since he'd come from New York, she didn't expect he'd been born to the saddle.

"When did you learn to ride?" Carly could feel her raised spirits getting set to take a dive.

"When I was a kid," Josh answered, certain he knew what she was thinking, since she was aware he hadn't been born a cowboy. "My grandparents have a farm in Rhode Island. Horses, cows, chickens." It was the truth, but Josh thought to himself that he probably would have fabricated it for her if it wasn't.

Gabby brought over a plate with two thick lamb chops done to perfection. Alongside the chops, artfully displayed, were freshly cooked carrots, string beans and a baked potato. He put the plate down in front of Carly. "Do you like butter or sour cream on your potato?"

"Butter." Carly gave Gabby a smile. "If I eat all this I won't have room to even taste the chili, and I do want to taste it. I've never tried chili before."

Billy Jack stuck his fork into the bowl of chili and held the filled fork up to Carly's mouth.

Carly accepted and all the men, including Josh, watched the fork slip between her lips and come out clean. Josh contemplated the pitcher of lemonade on the table. If he aimed his elbow right the pitcher might just fall into Billy Jack's lap. The guy looked as if he needed to be hosed down.

"I never thought I'd like chili. You're a wonderful cook," Carly told Gabby, hoping she was making it clear that she wasn't just saying it because it was expected.

Gabby pulled his chair out from the table and sat, looking as if he'd just been handed a chef's award. "Eat your lamb chops before they turn cold."

Carly put her fork and knife to her chops while the guys filled their bowls with chili. "Mmmm," Carly said as Gabby watched her chew her first bite. She hadn't eaten the other half of her sandwich from lunch and she'd poured the beer down the sink. She was starved now, and the lamb chop was out of this world.

"How about we all go into town tonight and hang out at Mother's?" Ben threw out the suggestion.

"Fine with me," Paulie answered.

Josh nodded his head in agreement.

Gabby, who turned in early every night, just went on eating.

"Carly, would you like to go?" Billy Jack asked. "Mother's is the only place in town that's hopping. They have music, dart boards, pool tables. Only it's not fancy or anything."

Carly hesitated, but not because she didn't like the idea of going. She didn't think that Josh would appreciate her tagging along.

"You'll be bored around here," Josh tossed out, looking as if he couldn't care less one way or the other. "You haven't seen anything of Poquotte Falls yet."

"Come on, Carly. Come with us," Ben coaxed earnestly.

"I'll teach you how to throw darts." Paulie wagged his eyebrows at her.

Carly took several small breaths. "Okay. I'd like to come along."

They continued with their dinners, talking about the weather and other topics. The men had more than one bowl of chili apiece. And Carly ate everything on her plate, trying to appease what felt like a bunch of crickets jumping around in her stomach.

Gabby got to his feet and Carly stood as well. "Let me help clean up," she said.

The older man shrugged Carly's offer aside. "The kitchen is my domain. You go do whatever you gals do to get ready for a night out."

She hadn't considered how she should dress. If there had been another woman going along it would have been simple enough to coordinate, but she was the only woman in this group. Since Billy Jack had been the first one to extend her an invitation, Carly asked, "How do women dress to go to Mother's?" Only it wasn't Billy Jack that she had in her sight. Carly's eyes had gone to Josh.

"You're dressed fine the way you are." His blue gaze swept over her without lingering. "You'll need a jacket. Your green one," he reminded her, "is in the hall closet."

Carly thought about how he'd kidded her earlier for putting her jacket over the moose. He wasn't being playful with her now. "I'll just freshen up. Give me a few minutes, okay?"

"Take your time." Josh lounged in his seat. "It's too early to go now. We'll meet you in front of the cabin around eight-thirty."

"Would you like me to walk you back to the cabin?" Billy Jack asked.

"I'm fine," Carly answered, and hurried off, though she'd just been given more than an hour to get ready.

Carly took most of the time trying to do something different with her hair, only to end up twisting it back into a topknot the way she'd had it to begin with. Her hair was just too wild and unruly to wear loose, and she was too tidy by nature to cope with that look on herself. She hated her hair, mostly because it was so red. She would have dyed it years ago if it wouldn't have hurt her father. His mother had been a redhead.

The men were all in front of the cabin when Carly came out. Startled, she stared at the pack of motorcycle hoods awaiting her in denim jackets and helmets. They were all straddling their bikes. Josh was the first in line, the leader of the gang. Billy Jack was right behind him, followed by Paulie, then Ben.

Carly hadn't given any thought to transportation. She remembered now that Denny Robbins had the Jeep. Not that they could have all fit in the Jeep anyway. Of course, lack of transportation, as Josh had put it when she'd first arrived, was the reason she'd wound up staying at the cabin.

She didn't dwell on the explanation Josh had given her for not being able to take her to a motel or the implication associated with it. Right now Carly was absorbed in the realization that she was expected to ride on the back of one of the bikes. Did she get to choose? She'd never been on a motorcycle.

Billy Jack swung off his bike and approached Carly, an extra helmet in his hand. He extended it to her. "Can't ride without one," he said, eyeing Carly's hair.

Carly accepted the helmet. Obviously, she wasn't going to get to choose whom she rode with. Carly put a smile on her face while she worked the helmet over her hair, dislodging some pins. Her eyes sought out Josh and noticed that he had an extra helmet hanging off his handlebar.

Billy Jack walked Carly over to his bike. "Just hop on behind me," he said, getting on first.

Carly could still feel some ache in her legs as she positioned herself behind Billy Jack. She was glad she'd decided not to take her shoulder bag with her. It would have got in her way now. She'd put her money in the pocket of her green blazer.

Billy Jack turned his head. "Bring your knees up and hold on to me."

Carly brought her knees up and wrapped her arms across Billy Jack's back. And they were off in a roar. Carly was so scared she could hardly breathe, but she was equally excited. Carly Gerard—biker chick!

Josh maneuvered his bike beside Billy Jack's after they'd turned off the highway to take the single-lane road to town. He motioned to Billy Jack to slow down. It was one thing for them to ride like bats out of hell when it was just the guys and the road to town was clear. Though the road was clear tonight, Billy Jack had Carly on his seat, hanging on tight. Josh bet this was the first time she'd ever been on a bike.

Billy Jack nodded agreeably to Josh and slowed down, a big smile on his face. Josh didn't know where the feeling was coming from or why he was having it, but he felt like punching Billy Jack's lights out.

It was just turning dark as Billy Jack, Carly and Josh pulled up in front of Mother's. Paulie and Ben had left the three in their dust a while back, but they were sitting on their bikes waiting. Country music was playing loud enough inside Mother's to be previewed outdoors. A neon sign lent a glare to the night air.

Carly backed herself off Billy Jack's bike, her hands to the portion of the seat she'd occupied giving herself some balance. She felt a little wobbly. Billy Jack got off his bike lickety-split, as did the rest of the guys. Carly wasn't aware of the moment Josh moved to her side—only that he was there. They walked to the door of Mother's, Carly sandwiched between Josh and Billy Jack.

Inside, the music was much louder now. Three musicians were singing and strumming guitars. Ben and

Paulie, not having shortened their pace to accommodate Carly as Billy Jack and Josh had, were already at the bar. Paulie was trying to attract one of the two bartenders, but there was quite a crowd. There were no empty stools.

"What are you having?" Paulie called out to Carly, after getting the attention of a bartender.

"A beer," Carly answered, trying to be one of the guys. "A light one if they have it." Light had to be better than the regular kind.

Carly put her hand in her pocket and took out five dollars to pass to Paulie. She had no idea how much a single bottle of beer cost, but she'd brought twenty dollars with her. Not that she had any intention of drinking her way through that amount.

"Put your money away," Paulie said, having to shout a little. "We guys are taking you out. I've got this round."

Carly was about to object, but Josh winked briefly at her, supporting Paulie's statement. It was Josh's declaration that Carly responded to without any objection. Carly Gerard, who had a hard enough time getting a single date, had four men taking her out at once.

"Do you know how to do the two-step?" Ben asked her after the bottles were passed out.

"No." Carly gazed at the group of line dancers in front of the bandstand. "Is that what they're doing out there?" Country and western dancing was the current craze in New York City. Carly knew some of the names of the dances, had even seen an ad on TV that offered a tape and instruction book for sale. But she'd never expected to find herself needing to know the "tushy-push."

Billy Jack, looking perturbed at Ben's attempt to get Carly out on the dance floor, threw out a different offer. "Carly, would you like to learn how to play pool?"

Actually, she knew how to play pool. Her brother Eddie had taught her and she was quite good at it. She beat Eddie every time they played, and he claimed he was a pro.

"I'd like to play pool," Carly replied, hoping Josh would join them, and hoping that Eddie hadn't been teasing her. She wanted to show off.

Not only did Josh come along, but so did Ben and Paulie.

The pool tables were in a separate room beyond an archway. The men went to the wall for cue sticks, Billy Jack getting one for Carly. The guys took off their denim jackets and hung them up on pegs. Carly transferred her money from her blazer pocket to her jeans pocket then took off her blazer and found a peg for herself. They had to wait a few minutes for a table to open up.

"Why don't the four of you play and let me watch first," Carly encouraged brightly as they headed to grab the table.

The guys put up five-dollar bets before they began to play. Billy Jack won against Ben. Josh won against Paulie. Josh was the best at the game. Still, there had been a shot Josh had missed that Carly thought she might have been able to pocket.

"Ready to try?" Josh asked, regarding Carly. Her hair was only precariously in place at this point.

"Yes," she answered enthusiastically.

"I'll show you how to hold the stick," Josh said, squeezing Billy Jack out just as the younger man was moving in.

Billy Jack didn't keep his disappointment from showing as Josh got behind Carly. There was a second when Carly considered telling Josh that she knew how to play pool. But she didn't.

Josh's arms came around her to set the cue stick properly in her hands and place her fingers the right way. Carly's breathing was rushed as she dealt with the intimacy of their entwined posture. He really did things to her. No doubt he did things to every female he came into contact with. Women probably threw themselves at his cowboy boots.

"Don't move," Josh said, stepping back from Carly. "Keep your hands and fingers just the way they are now. I'll break for you. Try to hit one of the balls. It doesn't matter which one."

"Okay." It was hard for Carly to get her body to stop quivering. "How much should we bet?"

Josh grinned. "I don't think you're ready for betting yet."

It was all she could do to try to look innocent. Carly Gerard, the biker chick, was hustling. "I think it would be more fun if we bet. You guys bet each other."

Josh's grin broadened. "How much do you want to bet?"

"Ten dollars." Carly guilelessly met Josh's grin head-on.

"You're sure?"

"I'm sure," she answered, testing the cue stick a little, letting it slide a bit through her fingers.

"You're going to make me feel like a bum taking money from you," Josh said.

Ben stuck his two cents in to champion her. "The game isn't over until the fat lady sings. I don't see any fat ladies around here."

Josh fixed his teasing blue eyes on Carly before he broke the balls. "Go to it."

Carly studied the lay of the balls on the table. Then taking a deep breath, she began to play. She sank the first ball she cued straight into the side pocket she'd aimed for. She didn't start calling her shots until after she had the table halfway cleared. By then, four mouths had dropped open.

"You . . ." Josh laughed as Carly polished off the table. "You hustled me!"

"Uh-huh," Carly proclaimed dramatically. Trying to keep a straight face, she wet her pointer finger with the tip of her tongue, held it up in the air and made a sizzling sound that came out like a whistle.

Grinning, Josh took out ten dollars and handed the bill to her. Carly made a big production out of stuffing it into her jeans pocket.

Josh tilted a cocky eyebrow. "Now that you're loaded, what do you say we make it twenty dollars this time. And we toss a coin to see who breaks."

"Twenty-five dollars and you're on, cowboy," Carly dared him back, discovering something wonderful. She, Carly Gerard, had some flippancy and brazenness deep down in her soul.

Josh couldn't stop smiling at her as he pulled a quarter out of his pocket. "Your call."

"Heads," Carly said, trying to look minxlike.

Josh threw the coin in the air. It landed tails up on the table. He sent her a sexy flick of his blue eyes.

"Don't let him intimidate you." Paulie smiled at Carly. "I've got twenty that says he'll miss and you'll mop up the table with him." Paulie turned from Carly to look for a taker to lay off his bet.

"My money is on Carly, too," Billy Jack said, trying to catch Carly's glance, but her eyes were now on Josh.

And he was holding on to her gaze.

"Don't look at me," Ben told the other two men. "I think she can beat the pants off him, too."

Not removing his eyes from the devilishness going on in Carly's, Josh said, "Thanks, guys."

"What can we say?" Paulie wisecracked to Josh. "We like her style."

"All right." Josh laughed. He was liking her style too. "I'll take you all on."

"Any time you're ready, cowboy," Carly bandied, flicking her yellow-green eyes at him the way he'd flicked his blue eyes at her.

Josh made a big deal out of chalking his stick, all the while keeping his sight on her mischievous gaze. He was reacting sexually to her and he knew it. How had the librarian-schoolmarm got him going like this?

Carly watched Josh break. She calculated the table he'd laid out for himself, but her mind wasn't fully on the game. Had he felt any of what she'd felt when he'd kissed her?

Josh worked half the table clear and was aiming for a shot that wasn't hard at all when it hit him. He didn't want to win. He didn't want to beat her at this.

"I didn't think you'd miss that one," Carly said in surprise, taking over the table. For a moment she wondered if he'd deliberately missed it, but she let the idea go to concentrate on her game.

"That's what I call an easy twenty," Paulie said, collecting from Josh after Carly won.

"Thanks for not rubbing it in." Josh grinned and handed a twenty to Ben, a twenty to Billy Jack and then twenty-five dollars to Carly.

"You didn't let me win, did you?" Carly asked suspiciously.

Josh feigned chagrin. "No way. You don't think I wanted to pay these bums off."

"How about you and me?" Billy Jack put himself between Carly and Josh.

"All right." Carly's eyes met Josh's as soon as Billy Jack moved out of her way to toss a coin on the table.

Carly beat Billy Jack, lost to Paulie and was just beginning a game with Ben when she heard Paulie say to Josh, "Hey, hey... Look who just came in."

Not only did Josh turn his head to look, but Carly looked as well, following the direction of Josh's gaze. What she saw was a gorgeous brunette with perfect long straight hair and a dynamite body. She'd come in with a man, but she left him and was heading toward them. Carly knew it was Josh she was singling out, not Billy Jack, Paulie or Ben.

"Hi, Alicia," Josh said idly as she came up in front of him.

"Josh." Alicia's gray eyes swept over Josh in a way that impressed the hell out of Carly. It was sort of a once-over, but sexier.

"It's your shot," Ben prompted Carly.

Distracted, Carly took quick aim and missed. She was more interested in what was going on between Josh and Alicia than she was in winning or losing a game of pool.

"I'm here with someone," Alicia said coolly.

Enviously Carly watched Alicia's hair swing with just a slight tilt of her head.

"I noticed," Josh said loosely.

The other woman put a well-placed hand on her hip. "I was going to call you and let you know it was over between us."

Oh, my God, Carly thought. They'd been going together and now she was dumping him. Getting dumped was bad enough. Getting dumped in front of the guys and in front of her had to be just awful for him. What was wrong with this woman anyway? Was she crazy?

Josh shrugged indifferently. "Well, I guess you saved yourself the cost of a call."

So this was the way the male ego worked, Carly evaluated. Cool. Very cool.

"Well, I'll see you around," Alicia said, already in a half turn.

"Right. Take care," Josh replied easily.

"I'll take twenty," Ben was saying to Carly.

It was a second before Carly realized what Ben was talking about. Then it came to her that Ben had just won their game. She took out twenty dollars and gave it over to him.

Josh stretched his shoulders and chest. "I don't know about the rest of you, but I'm beat. I'm going to head back."

Carly watched Josh go for his jacket and put it on. Ben was talking about the four of them choosing pairs and playing another game.

Josh was just outside the archway to the main room of the bar when Carly grabbed her blazer. "Well, I'm tired. Bushed." She spoke in a quick clip. "I'll go back with Josh." Carly was certain that Josh needed someone to talk to.

Josh was already on his bike, placing his helmet on his head, when Carly raced over and jumped on behind him.

He squared a look back at her. Not saying anything, he took the extra helmet off the bar of his bike and held it out to her. Carly put it on and then wound her arms tight across his back. She was about to say something soothing to him, but he was already bouncing to put the bike in motion. And then she couldn't speak because of the wind in her face.

The excitement Carly had felt riding with Billy Jack paled drastically compared to the excitement she felt riding with Josh. She wished they had a hundred miles to go.

All too soon for Carly, Josh brought the bike to a stop in front of the cabin. Carly reluctantly alighted and took off the helmet. He accepted it from her, and strapped it back on the bar of his bike.

"Why didn't you have Billy Jack bring you back?" Josh asked, taking off his own helmet.

"I wanted to talk to you." But Carly wasn't quite sure what to say now that they were alone.

"About what?"

"I...ah... I wanted to tell you not to feel bad about Alicia. You can get any number of women."

Josh grinned. "Can I get you?" he asked teasingly. Only as soon as he put the quip out, Josh became edgy and wrought up.

Carly knew he was kidding around. "As a partner," she answered flippantly.

Josh quirked a wink. "You're getting real sharp there with those comebacks."

"Thanks." Carly gave Josh an impertinent glance and then started toward the porch. She stopped on the first step and turned back to him. "You are sleeping in the bunkhouse, right?"

He agitatedly ran his hands through his hair. "Yeah, where elsc?"

Chapter Seven

Carly listened for a moment, certain she was hearing someone walking around in the living room. After getting out of bed to investigate, she came face-to-face with Josh outside her room.

"I realized I needed a clean shirt," he told her. "Did I wake you?"

"No." Carly's head went from side to side. It was the only part of her that moved. "I wasn't sleeping yet."

He'd turned on one of the lamps and she could see his blue eyes slowly scan her body. "So you sleep in pajamas, huh?"

"Yes." Carly glanced down at herself, taking in her totally unsexy brown-and-white pin-striped flannel pajamas. Why didn't she own a nightgown? Why didn't she own a sexy nightie?

"Well, I'll just go get a shirt." He started to walk around her, then his eyes met hers and he stopped in front of her.

She didn't know how long they stayed like that with their eyes locked. She was suddenly very warm—unbelievably warm. Carly thought of her loose curly hair turning frizzy as it did when the humidity got high, but the thought didn't remain in her head for long.

She made the first move. Leaning forward into a precision-perfect free fall, she flung her arms around his neck. All on her own, she kissed him. But she wasn't on her own for very long. Before she could even feel any amazement at her unprecedented action, he was kissing her back and setting off sparks.

He brought her up closer, but there wasn't any force involved. It was more a lazy kind of movement. His hands went to her hips. His chest came to her chest. His denim jacket was stiff against the soft fabric of her pajama top. Carly felt the instant he became fully aroused.

He removed his mouth from hers just long enough for them both to catch a breath, and then his lips were back again and this time his tongue moved wet and warm along her teeth. Given a turn, Carly placed her tongue to his teeth and then even more brazen than he'd been, she sought further access. She tasted beer and thought he might have had more to drink in the bunkhouse after he'd left her outside the cabin. She liked the way the beer tasted in his mouth.

"Whew," he said when they broke apart again. "You're good at this."

Confidently Carly smiled. "Yes, but you're better."

"I'm really hot, Carly."

"Why don't you take your jacket off," she said, and then realized that wasn't what he'd meant.

He kidded her by pretending to consider her suggestion. Looking at her with the tease still in his eyes, he finally took off his jacket and let it fall from his hand. His eyes became suddenly serious. "I wasn't looking for this to happen."

She was going to say, "I was," but she didn't. After a convulsive gulp, she whispered, "I know."

"We can stop right now," he murmured, already flattening her body back against his.

"Don't stop," Carly said wantonly. "Please, don't stop."

She didn't know how they got down on the carpet with him stretched over her. But it was incredibly sensuous even to just lie there beneath him without him doing anything at all. He started placing kisses along her neck as he raised one of her legs over his hip bringing them as near to joining intimately as they could possibly get with him in jeans and her in pajamas. The need he was generating made Carly draw in choppy, trembling breaths.

He rolled a little onto his side and his fingers worked open the buttons of her pajama top. Instinctively Carly brought an arm up to cover herself as quickly as he exposed her to his gaze. She'd always felt that her breasts were okay, but the rest of her was skin and bones.

"Don't you want me to look at you and touch you there?" His irises were a smoky, smoldering sexy blue.

"Josh…" She hadn't intended to hamper him. She didn't want to stop him. She was wild for him to do anything he wanted to do with her and was reservedly uncomfortable all at the same time. A picture of Alicia's much more curvaceous body flitted through her head.

"I won't do anything you don't want me to do." His voice was husky. "Is it okay if I unbutton my shirt?"

She wanted to do it for him. She wanted to do so very much. "Can I open it for you?"

"Sure." He smiled at her—that sexy-as-hell smile.

Her arm came down and her fingers went to the buttons of his denim shirt. When she could go no farther than the buckle of his belt, he accommodated her by yanking his shirt free from his jeans. With her eyes on his consummately male muscular chest, Carly opened the last of the buttons.

He ran his fingers through her hair. She thought he said something about liking her hair free, but she wasn't sure. By then she'd placed her mouth to his chest and was kissing him there. Her tongue glanced across one of his nipples and he groaned. Liking that, Carly went and did it again—slower this time. His body shuddered. The realization that she, Carly Gerard, was causing him to respond in such a way stole her breath away. She had never before felt this kind of thrill. She was dizzy with delight.

"Let me do that to you. Please, Carly." His words were low and thick, said as if he were having trouble getting them out.

She lifted her head, and it was all the permission he needed. He could easily read in her eyes the delirious wanting there. Carly could see it for herself as if she were two separate people and was viewing what was happening to her.

The look of the two of them was so incredibly provocative it made her squirm. She squirmed even more as he removed her pajama top and lowered his head. His tongue cruised first one nipple then the other, while the edges of his teeth rode lightly over each crested point. She became too mindless to hold the image of how they looked together as her mind and body gave in to a stronger demand.

"Carly, I think I've fallen in love with you," he gasped. His eyes, as he looked into her face, were smoldering even more than before. "I didn't want to fall in love with you. I really didn't.... I didn't even know it was happening. How did you do this to me?"

Carly smiled. She wanted to pat herself on the back. "I needed to make you love me, because I love you. I love you, Josh. I love you, I love you, I love you...."

Carly's eyelids flashed open. It took a few seconds for her to focus. She'd fallen asleep with the lamp on and she could see around the bedroom—more clearly as she became more fully awake. The magazine she'd been reading before she'd fallen asleep fell to the floor as she sprang up to a sitting position. Carly's heart was beating so hard she thought it might explode. She looked at the clock, and saw that two hours had passed since she'd come back with Josh from Mother's. She groaned and buried her head into her pillow.

* * *

When Carly woke again it was nearly noon. It had taken her forever to fall back asleep. She'd drunk two mugs of hot milk—her mother's cure for sleeplessness. She'd taken a cold shower, wondering why that worked for men and not women. All it did was make her shiver. She'd had to take a hot shower to stop shaking. After that, she'd exercised vigorously with as much coordination as she could until she'd finally worn herself out.

She didn't hear anyone in the cabin as she stepped out of the bedroom with a terry-cloth robe tied tightly about her waist. Just the thought of facing Josh filled Carly with embarrassment. Of course, he'd have no way of knowing what she'd dreamed about, but the memory was still fresh in her mind.

She didn't have to worry. He wasn't in the kitchen, though he'd left her a note on the table.

Sleepy head,

Gabby's got brunch going in the kitchen until noon. Whatever time you wake up, I know Gabby will be more than happy to make sure you're well-fed. See you,

                                          Josh.

Gabby was bustling in the kitchen of the mess hall when Carly arrived dressed in a gray man-tailored shirt and jeans. She'd already made herself something to eat—coffee and toast. It was going on one o'clock.

"Howdy, little gal," Gabby greeted effusively, without any stop to his activity. He was adding ingredients to a large pot of brown liquid cooking on the stove. "I've got a turkey sandwich waiting for you in the refrigerator, with a helping of my special macaroni salad. Take it out and eat."

"I've eaten already. Thank you." Carly smiled. "What are you making now?"

"I'm putting together my sauce for chicken and ribs. We're going to have a barbecue after the show. Give you a chance to meet everyone. It will be too hectic for you now with getting the show on. Hope you like the idea."

Smiling, Carly nodded her head. She was thrilled with the idea. "Is it Josh's idea?" She was certain it was.

"Actually it was Paulie who came up with it."

After a long moment of feeling disappointed, Carly asked, "Where is Paulie and everyone else?" She didn't want to even mention Josh now.

"Paulie and Josh are checking on the horses and props. Ben and Billy Jack are out back shucking ears of corn for tonight. Denny took the Jeep into town to pick up the ribs and chicken. Everyone else is down at the set doing whatever they need to do to get ready for the show. The women use the saloon to get into their costumes. You might want to go on down there."

"What can I do to help you here?" Carly wanted to be occupied.

"I've got it all under control. Why don't you go find Josh? I'm sure he'd like for you to see how everything gets set up."

Carly imagined that the last thing Josh wanted was to have her underfoot. Then again, they had got along very nicely when they'd been at Mother's. And she was his partner, whether he liked it or not. She had gumption, didn't she?

It was an hour before Carly even noticed Josh, and by then the stadium seats were three-quarters filled, as filled as they were going to get with the show about to begin. She'd met a number of the people who worked the show. She'd been easily picked out as the new partner in their midst. She'd been pleasantly, though hurriedly, welcomed as everyone went about their work.

Carly saw Josh walk behind the backdrop of the staged Western town. Before she even thought to cross in front of the audience to follow him and find out what she should be doing, a group of Native Americans had come out to center stage. Staying where she was at the sideline, Carly watched wide-eyed as the group began to dance, chant and beat tom-toms.

A voice came across a loudspeaker. "Welcome to the greatest, most authentic, Wild West show in America. Let's give a big Oklahoma cheer for Chief Big Horn and his rattlesnake dance."

The applause came, then quieted as Chief Big Horn stepped forward. He drew a rattlesnake out of a box, and held it up over his head while the snake hissed. The tom-toms began again and the chief danced with the snake coiled around his neck.

As did the audience, Carly watched in fascination as each act of the show unfolded. There were lasso jumpers and daredevil stunts. Denny, as Jesse James, robbed the "bank" and along with his gang jumped on horses for their getaway, followed by a posse of riders. The Earp brothers and Doc Holliday came up against Ike Clanton and company for a gunfight in Tombstone. The show's new Buffalo Bill challenged Annie Oakley to shoot bull's-eye shots with him at a large target. The crowd laughed at Annie Oakley's antics as she won over a very annoyed Buffalo Bill. Carly was laughing, too. She had moved to a seat, wanting a better view of all that was going on.

The smile still on her face, Carly heard the announcer introduce Butch Cassidy and the Sundance Kid along with a small band of riders. Carly picked out Billy Jack in the group as a stagecoach rolled into town. Paulie and Ben stopped the coach and four ladies in costumes stepped out. Butch and Sundance charmingly robbed the women of their purses, while flirting outrageously with the audience's approval. As soon as all the actors cleared the area, the announcer spoke again. "Here comes Calamity Jane bringing in the mail. Isn't that Wild Bill Hickok riding in after her?"

Carly held her breath. She saw the Pony Express wagon with Calamity Jane seated in the box seat. The woman playing Calamity Jane had long blond hair tied loosely at the nape of her neck with a strip of rawhide. She was wearing a tan-colored shirt and pants—both fringed. Then Carly saw Josh as Wild Bill rein in his horse just as Calamity Jane stopped the wagon. Carly's eyes stayed on Josh. He had his Western hat on and a period-styled bluish-gray suit with a white shirt and drawstring necktie held in place by a turquoise and silver medallion. Carly didn't know what Wild Bill Hickok was famous for, but if it had anything to do with sex appeal, he was being played to perfection by the cowboy she was looking at.

Josh agilely alighted from his horse. "Need a hand coming down, Calamity?" he drawled while he gave the blonde a seductively tantalizing look.

"I can get down all by myself." The actress hammed it up for the audience in a Mae West kind of voice. "But I sure wouldn't want to spoil your reputation as a *gentleman.*"

Carly's gaze remained fixed on Josh as he put his hands to Calamity's waist and brought her down from the top of the buckboard. It was just the way Carly remembered him bringing her down from Lady Luck. Only he didn't do any funny business with his hands at Calamity's waist the way he'd done to her when he'd slid his hands up to within a millimeter of her breasts. Carly took a very deep breath and tried to settle herself. It didn't work.

"So, Calamity, did you shoot any bad guys along the way this trip?" Wild Bill teased.

Calamity Jane placed her hands on her hips and pushed her chest out. Carly regarded her competitively. The woman playing the role of Calamity Jane was tall and pretty—very pretty. Late twenties at most. Carly pathetically tallied up her own shortcomings in comparison. Being even taller than Calamity Jane was just one of them.

"Only about ten this time," the actress bragged. "Had to use two rifles—one in each hand."

"One in each hand," Wild Bill repeated, tossing a grin to the crowd.

"Don't you go sassing me, Wild Bill," Calamity Jane countered. "That's no way to treat a lady."

"A lady!" Wild Bill laughed. "You sure don't look like any lady I've ever seen."

"I can look like a lady anytime I want to look like a lady," Calamity Jane retorted, all huffy.

"I'd have to see it to believe it." Josh winked at the crowd.

Carly tried to catch Josh's eye, but not for long. Her attention quickly went back to Calamity Jane as the blonde began taking off her shirt to reveal a studded and fringed pink midriff top. The slacks came off next—pull-away slacks that she whipped off easily to reveal a short skirt that matched her top. As she strutted around in white Western boots showing her stuff to Wild Bill and the audience, Calamity Jane pulled the rawhide strip from her hair letting her thick blond mane fly free. The crowd broke into raucous hoots, howls and whistles. Josh hammed it up, taking his jacket off and fanning his face with his hand. It was great fun and Carly could see it as that, but it didn't stop her from feeling envious.

Calamity Jane wiggled her hips in front of Josh. "Think you might be fixing to make an honest woman of me one of these days?"

"Maybe one of these days." Josh grinned broadly. "Right now that's not quite what I'm fixing to do." As he spoke, Josh put his arm around Calamity Jane and assisted her up into the wagon portion of the Pony Express. He vaulted in right after her.

For a moment they were concealed from the audience's view. Then Calamity Jane raised her head over the sideboard. "Now I know why they call you *Wild Bill*," she told the still riotous crowd.

The announcer's voice came over the loudspeaker. "Thank you all for coming. Tell your friends and come again."

The Native Americans returned with tom-toms going. One of the group got up on the box seat of the Pony Express and rode it around to the rear of the town. Another mounted Wild Bill Hickok's horse and followed the wagon.

Carly looked at her watch as the audience began leaving their seats and heading for the parking lot. The show had begun at two-thirty. It was now almost five.

She wanted to tell Josh how much she'd loved the show, but she didn't get the opportunity. As soon as the last of the cars left the parking field, Gabby began setting the barbecue up. Carly insisted on helping. Josh, Billy Jack, Ben, Paulie and Denny did their share. With all the mingling going on while everyone ate, Carly didn't get a chance to catch Josh alone.

Josh came into the mess hall just as Carly put away the last pot she'd washed and dried. It was nine o'clock. She'd talked Gabby into turning in and letting her finish cleaning up on her own.

"I'll go back to the cabin with you," Josh said. "I need to pick up a few things."

"I've been wanting to tell you all night how great the show is," Carly said. But her mind wasn't on the show at the moment. She was remembering the dream she'd had about him, and how it had started with him coming to the cabin to pick up a clean shirt.

"I'm glad that you liked it." He didn't understand why it should matter to him whether she'd liked the show or not. But he was suddenly pleased.

"I loved it," Carly affirmed, putting on the blazer she'd gone to the cabin for during the evening. She was struggling to apply every ounce of common sense she could dredge up to keep her thoughts straight.

"I liked your skit the best," Carly added as they left the bunkhouse. She was glad there wasn't much lighting. She could feel that her face was heated. *Get your act together. Will you, please!* She admonished herself.

"Betsy Sue does a good job," Josh remarked.

"She's very pretty." Carly had made sure she met Betsy Sue Miller, the woman who portrayed Calamity Jane.

"Yes," Josh agreed as they neared the cabin.

"She's very nice, too." Carly had been looking to find some fault with the woman, but she hadn't found any. Betsy Sue was warm, friendly and charming. Betsy Sue wasn't just a man's kind of woman, she was an all-around nice person, too.

"Did you ever date Betsy Sue?" Carly queried, trying to sound conversational.

"No," Josh answered as they climbed the stairs to the porch of the cabin. He didn't bother taking his boots off, but wiped his soles on the mat instead. Carly did the same.

"I suppose you don't feel you should mix business with pleasure," Carly commented as Josh opened the door and the two of them came into the living room.

"I don't have a problem with that," Josh said lightly. "But I don't think Betsy Sue's husband would approve of her dating."

"Oh," Carly breathed and then scooted her eyes away from his teasing gaze.

"Well, I guess I should get my things." He was suddenly feeling very restless.

"Right." Carly was feeling very awkward. *If he stops in front of me and looks into my eyes, I'm going to faint.*

The phone rang just as Josh headed for his bedroom. He changed direction and went to the kitchen to pick it up.

"It's your mother," Josh called out to Carly a moment later.

She entered the kitchen and took the receiver from his hand.

Josh found Carly back in the living room when he came out of his bedroom with a knapsack. "Everything okay with your mom?" he asked.

"Yes." Carly smiled. "I know I shouldn't have mentioned I was learning to ride a horse. My mother has probably got my father checking information now for the names of all the orthopedists in the area. I don't think she took my word that I don't have any part of myself in a cast. Thank God she got another call and had to get off the phone with me." Carly raised her eyes to the ceiling as if thanking the powers above.

Josh grinned and dropped the knapsack he'd filled with some clothing on the couch. "Would you like me to call and reassure her that you're okay?"

Carly shook her head and smiled. "She'd find that very suspicious. You wouldn't be able to convince my mother not to worry. She'll have my father crazy by the morning. They both know how uncoordinated I am."

"You don't seem uncoordinated to me." He was enjoying the engagingly comical things she was doing with her eyes.

"You don't have enough experience with me yet." Carly could tell he was getting a kick out of her. She had no problem with that. "I'm truly a klutz." Carly intentionally rolled her eyes, as eye gestures seemed to appeal to him. "I've always been a klutz. When I was eight years old my mother took me out of dancing school because I kept tripping over my feet. She was sure I was going to hurt myself."

Josh felt a pull of his heart and a strong desire to put his arms around her. "Were you very disappointed to leave dancing school?"

"I was relieved." Carly grinned. "It didn't bother me that I was always tripping over myself. I wasn't the only one. The part I hated about dancing lessons were the recitals when I had to dance with a boy. I was the only girl that was two heads taller than every boy in the class."

Josh's concern that she'd been hurt at having been taken out of dancing school was replaced by cowboy devilry. "How do you feel about dancing with a guy that tops you by at least an inch?" He'd already determined that he was at least that much taller than her.

"Well . . ." Carly was thrown by his question.

"Come on. I feel like dancing."

"Now?" Carly swallowed. "Where?"

"Now. Here." The look he gave her was enticingly sexy.

Carly could feel her knees turning to jelly. Was he flirting with her? "There's no music."

Josh walked over to the stereo system against one wall and turned the FM radio on. He tuned in a country and western ballad. "There's music now."

Carly took a number of long breaths, trying to find her sense of balance. But her sense of balance wasn't anywhere to be found.

"Take your blazer off," Josh said, shrugging out of his denim jacket and throwing it on one of the armchairs.

Carly took her blazer off. Instead of just dropping it over his jacket, which was her first inclination, Carly walked on shaky legs to the closet near the front door. She took her time hanging up her jacket.

With nothing more to do at the closet, Carly came back to Josh, but not right up to him. He had to take the few steps needed to bring her into his arms.

Carly could just about make out that a new ballad had begun. It was hard for her to hear the music clearly. Her pulse was beating too loudly in her ears.

Josh moved left. Carly moved right.

He smiled. "I think only one of us can lead."

"It should be you," Carly uttered absurdly. She was wooden. Her feet didn't know where to go. Uncoordinated was too mild a word for the fumbling she was doing.

"Close your eyes and put your head on my shoulder," Josh suggested.

"Why?" Carly's head went backward instead of forward.

Josh grinned into her eyes. "I think you'll relax better that way."

Bringing herself nearer to him was hardly a way for her to relax. But doing anything other than what he'd suggested would have seemed ridiculous.

Carly closed her eyes and put her forehead to his shoulder. He had one arm about her waist, his other was down at her side along with hers. He laced their fingers together.

Carly used her free hand to hold on to his forearm. He hadn't pressed her against him. Their bodies were just barely touching, but it was more than enough to create widespread chaos in Carly.

"That's better," Josh murmured in her ear. "Are you an only child?" He was thinking about her overprotective parents, and he wanted to prove to her that she could dance comfortably with a guy if she wanted to.

"I have a brother three and a half years older than me. He taught me to play pool. My parents turned the basement into a rec room when we were in our teens. They put in a pool table. My brother never let me play against any of his friends, but we played pool together a lot." Carly could hear that she was speaking in a rush. She was keeping up with her heart as it reached an optimal runner's range. "I haven't played for a long time, not until last night."

"I plan to play pool with you again." Josh put his leg between her knees to better direct her into following his lead.

Carly was almost certain that she gave some accepting indication with her head that she was more than willing to play pool with him. It was impossible for her to focus on anything other than his leg moving between her.

"Were you in love with the guy on the elevator?"

"Stan?" Carly's eyes flew open and her head came up.

"If that's his name." Josh looked into her face.

She tried unsuccessfully to recall the exact kind of emotions she'd experienced with Stan. "We seemed to be very much alike. I thought we were right together."

"Is that what you call love?" He dipped her a little and raised her back up. Had she moaned with Stan the Elevator Man the way she'd moaned in her sleep?

"I suppose there's got to be more to love than that. I do believe in being sensible about love."

"Close your eyes," Josh whispered as Carly got her feet mixed up. He closed his own eyes for a second, but then opened them quickly after an image of her draped only in a towel came into his head.

Carly put her head back to his shoulder and tried to pay attention to her feet. Why had she said she believed in being sensible about love? What in heaven's name did that mean?

"If you really want to learn to ride Lady Luck you should let me give you lessons. I can teach you better than Billy Jack."

Carly lifted her head and looked him in the eye. "I didn't think you'd want to give me lessons. You don't even want us to stay partners."

"This has nothing to do with us staying partners." He didn't know what it *had* to do with, and he wasn't interested in questioning himself.

"Okay," Carly said hastily, her mind racing. If he was willing to give her riding lessons that had to mean he wasn't going to bring up a discussion about buying her out for at least as long as it took for her to learn to ride. Maybe she'd grow on him by then.

Josh twirled Carly around. "Actually I was a little riled that you went off without even asking me if I was willing to teach you." He hadn't realized he'd been riled until now.

"You were?" Carly stepped on his toe and blushed. "I'm sorry."

Josh smiled teasingly. "Is that an apology for not asking me to teach you?"

Though she'd apologized for stepping on his toe, Carly acquiesced to his prompting. "Yes." She was willing to say anything he wanted to hear.

Josh put the hand he'd had on the small of her back up to the topknot of her hair. A couple of hairpins came out and fell through his fingers. Without thinking about what he was doing, he took the rest of the hairpins out and tossed them to the floor. When he was finished, he ran his hand into her unrestricted hair. "You should wear your hair loose," he said.

Carly held her breath for so long, she might have turned blue if she hadn't also been blushing. "Are we still dancing?" she asked hesitantly when she'd just about begun to breathe again. Their bodies were still moving, but the music had stopped. There was a commercial on the radio now, though Carly couldn't make out the words.

"Do you want to stop?" He looked into her fantastic eyes.

"No..." She didn't want him to stop doing whatever it was he was doing. There wasn't a single sensible thought in her head.

Josh used his hand still linked with her hand to bring her hips closer in line with his. His other hand remained tangled in her hair.

He was going to kiss her! Carly was almost certain she was reading that in his eyes. A man couldn't possibly look at a woman the way he was looking at her and not mean to kiss her. Their faces were even in the right position, though Carly angled hers just a little to the left to be sure. It was the most she could think to do to encourage him.

Josh wanted to kiss her. He knew *she* wanted him to kiss her. He could have done it and called it a night.

But he needed to understand what he was feeling for her. Was it simple lust? Because that was the only kind of emotion he was willing to deal with.

Carly wished she could take the initiative as she had done in her dream. But this wasn't a fantasy. This was real life. There wasn't any way she could make the first move.

Josh untangled his fingers from her hair, and then let go of her other hand while Carly's heart dropped to her stomach. She couldn't do anything to change his mind. It was like dancing. He had to be the one to take the lead.

"I'd better let you get to sleep. You must be tired. I know I am." He was also experiencing something akin to panic.

At a loss, Carly watched Josh grab his jacket. "Will you give me a riding lesson tomorrow?" she asked.

"You'd have to be up early," Josh muttered. "Very early. Around six." He avoided looking at her. He wanted to get away. He wanted to take back his offer to give her riding lessons.

"I'll be up," she said as Josh made a quick path to the door.

Carly stared miserably at his retreating back. It wasn't until he closed the door behind him that she noticed he'd forgotten his knapsack. Carly raced to the door.

He was on the last step leading off the porch. "You forgot your knapsack," she called to him.

Josh turned and with a heavy sigh, came back up the stairs.

Chapter Eight

"Carly, I don't know what to do about you," Josh groaned as they stood in the living room.

He couldn't stop looking at her. He knew darn well what he wanted to do about her.

"Josh..." she whispered.

His hands found her waist, drawing her forward as he went backward. Suddenly they were sitting on the couch and he had her on his lap. He kissed that little beauty mark of hers that held all sorts of fascination for him. He kissed her lips hotly and boldly, not holding anything back. There was a ball of heat catapulting through his entire body.

She kept one arm tightly circled around his neck while she timidly touched his chest between the buttons of his shirt. The unsure play of her fingers brought another groan to him as he released her lips.

"Listen to me, Carly. Okay?" He was begging. "I can't just kiss you. I can't just touch you. Do you understand what I'm saying?"

"Yes." Her voice was breathy. "I want you to make love to me. I want to make love to you. Will you teach me how to be with you?"

"Oh, Carly..." Josh groaned, settling his mouth back on hers.

She looked into his face when he released her lips. "I've never felt this way. Not ever."

"Not with Stan?" He began to unbutton her shirt.

"Not with anyone." She said it very intently. "Can I tell you something?"

"You can tell me anything."

"I've been going crazy wanting you to be with me like this."

"I've been going crazier." Josh shuddered and groaned. "Out of my mind crazy...."

"Are you sick?" Paulie, still in jeans and a denim jacket having just come in, nudged Josh.

Josh shot up out of the bed, coming fully awake in an instant. He was in the bunkhouse. Carly was nowhere to be found.

Paulie put on a lamp. "You were groaning. Have you got a fever or something?"

"No," Josh answered, extremely uncomfortable. His body was heated up, but he hadn't come down with something that could be cured by a couple of aspirin.

"You sure?" Paulie questioned.

"Yes, I'm sure." Josh heard his tone come across sharper than he meant it to be.

"Sorry I woke you up then," Paulie apologized.

"Actually you did me a favor. You know how it is when you have things on your mind. They wind up haunting you in your sleep."

"What have you got on your mind?" Paulie asked.

"Just things." Josh pushed his fingers through his hair. "Nothing I can't handle." This was one for the books! The last time he'd had such an erotic dream he'd been in his teens.

"Is it about Carly?" Paulie took off his jacket.

"Carly?" Josh said her name awkwardly. "Why would it be about Carly?"

"The partnership," the other man clarified. "Aren't you still bugged about the partnership?"

"I'm not bugged. I don't let women bug me." Josh abruptly got out of bed. It didn't look to him like Paulie was planning to turn in yet. He hadn't made any move to take off his shirt or his jeans. Josh pulled on his jeans and walked out of the bedroom bare-chested, hoping to leave his friend behind.

Paulie followed him to the mess hall.

Josh went to the refrigerator and took out a beer. He wasn't in the mood for a beer, but he needed some reason for having come into the kitchen.

"Want one?" Josh cocked a look over at Paulie, who was sitting at the table.

"I've had my quota." He stretched back in his seat.

Josh came to the table with his beer, turned a chair and straddled it.

"I don't know why you won't concede that it might work out." Paulie rubbed his jaw. "I was there the other day when Jimmy Blatts told you she was doing a dynamite job with the bookkeeping. You know you don't want to be bothered with paperwork."

Josh thumbed the cap off his beer.

"I don't see her even trying to call any of the shots," Paulie went on. "What's she doing wrong?"

"What are you doing? Starting a fan club for her?" Josh brought the beer to his mouth and took a swallow. She had him constantly keyed up.... That was what she was doing wrong.

"How many women can you name that would be willing to pitch in to help clean out a stable?" Paulie provoked.

"Did I let her do it? No." Josh defended himself.

"What are you saying?" Paulie pinned a look at Josh. "That she just offered knowing you wouldn't let her do it?"

"Oh, she would have done it," Josh said testily. "She was annoyed that I didn't let her do it."

Vindicated, Paulie nodded his head. "You should have come with us to Mother's tonight. Ben got her out on the dance floor and taught her the two-step. Once she had it down, she didn't want to quit. She wore us all out taking turns dancing with her."

It struck Josh then that neither Ben, Billy Jack or Denny had returned to the bunkhouse. Were the three of them still at Mother's dancing with her?

Josh waited a second for Paulie to volunteer that information. He didn't.

Josh had to ask, "Are the guys still at Mother's with her?" Just whose bike was she going to come back on?

"They're still there, but I brought her back." Paulie grinned. "This was cute.... I order her a beer when we first get there and she tugs on my arm and asks if she'd look out of place if she drank a glass of wine. She doesn't really like beer. She was just trying to be one of us."

Josh gave a nod of his head. A dumb boost-to-his-ego kind of nod. He'd been right that she preferred wine. He knew her better than any of them.

"She was disappointed that you didn't come along." Paulie delivered that information with a lift to one eyebrow.

"Really?" Intent on seeming uninterested, Josh took another gulp of beer. Then he waited impatiently again for Paulie to elaborate. Finally, Josh asked, "Did she say she was disappointed?"

"She didn't say it, but I had the feeling that she was. Come to think of it, it's been looking to me like you've been going out of your way to avoid being around her." Paulie arched his eyebrow again.

"I do not go out of my way to avoid her." Josh stood his ground. "I give her riding lessons every morning. I've been giving her riding lessons for nearly three weeks now."

"I saw her on Lady Luck the other morning. It looks like she's got the hang of it. You think she still needs lessons?"

Josh was beyond ticked off. It was partly because of the way Paulie was focusing on him with his one eyebrow raised. "She's still afraid to try dismounting on her own. I'm not going to let her do it until she feels more confident."

"If you want I can take over for you. Maybe I can give her the confidence she needs. We get along real well. Real well."

"I'll get her there," Josh replied with an intensity that offset the edges of his teeth.

"Well . . ." Paulie raised his shoulders. "I'm gonna turn in. You going back to bed?"

"Not yet." Josh had a traitorously agitated feeling that if he closed his eyes right now he would pick up on that dream he'd been having and finish it.

"Your hair looks fantastic," Betsy Sue said to Carly as they stepped out of Poquotte Falls's one beauty parlor. "I told you Ellie was a genius with hair."

Carly slid her fingers through her new hairdo. Her hair still fell to her shoulder blades and was still curly and wavy. The difference was that the layered cut had made it miraculously manageable. In the past, she hadn't allowed any beautician to do more than trim the ends. It had been difficult to forget the haircut she'd had in her teens that had left her looking like Little Orphan Annie—except that she hadn't been little.

"You are a terrific friend. Thank you for talking me into doing it." Carly smiled. She'd been letting her hair go free since Josh had said he liked it loose, even though she thought it was a mess flying loose. He hadn't once said again that he liked her hair down. He barely said anything to her at all.

"By the end of today you are not going to recognize yourself," Betsy Sue declared as they headed for a small country-style restaurant just up the street.

They'd already decided to have lunch in town before driving to Tulsa for a day of shopping. It was nearly noon and they were both hungry.

"I'd be happy to buy into that idea," Carly replied.

"Your problem is that you need attitude," Betsy Sue lectured.

"I know what you're saying." Carly sighed. "It's getting it and holding on to it that's the hard part."

Betsy Sue opened the door to the restaurant. There couldn't have been more than a dozen tables, each arranged to seat four. The narrow dining room was beautifully paneled in a light veneer, scored with shelves of colorful knickknacks and lots of real greenery. Carly noticed a slice of a sparkling kitchen through an opening in the back wall.

There wasn't any hostess. Carly and Betsy Sue selected seating on their own, heading for a table by a window with tieback blue-and-white checkered curtains that matched the tablecloths. There were a few other women having lunch. It wasn't the kind of place one would expect to find cowboys.

"You have to take advantage of your assets." Betsy Sue went on talking while getting a wave of greeting from the one and only waitress and giving a wave back. "How do you expect to get Josh over the edge if you're not going to give him a push?"

"Josh?" Carly almost stammered—would have stammered if she'd had more than one syllable to get out. "You don't think that I'm interested in Josh? Where would you get an idea like that?"

The waitress, young and vivacious with honey-brown hair worn becomingly short, came over to their table with menus and a basket of hot rolls.

Betsy Sue held back her response to Carly and spoke to the waitress. "Hi, Maddie. This is Carly Gerard. Carly, this is Maddie Brooks. Maddie and I have been friends since high school, when she moved here to Poquotte Falls. We were both cheerleaders at Westlake High. Maddie's mother opened this restaurant a few years ago."

"Hi." Maddie gave Carly a delightful smile. "Your uncle was a real nice man. How do you like it over at the show?"

"I love it." Carly smiled back.

"Guess who called me this morning?" Maddie gave Betsy Sue the question.

Betsy Sue didn't take any time to think about it. "Paulie," she guessed.

"Yes." Maddie smiled again. "Did he say anything to you?"

Betsy Sue, sharing Maddie's grin, shook her head. "What did he say to you?"

"He asked if I wanted to go to a movie over in Westlake this coming Saturday night."

"And you said?" Betsy Sue asked.

"I said I *might* be interested in going to a movie Saturday night." Maddie gave a sparkling flash of her chestnut-brown eyes, contradicting the contrived impassive manner of speech she was using. "I told him to call me on Thursday and I'd let him know for sure."

"I love it." Betsy Sue gave Maddie a thumbs-up sign.

"Me, too." Maddie put down the bread basket and handed out the two menus she'd brought with her.

"Maddie's mom makes a dynamite grilled chicken salad with honey-mustard sauce," Betsy Sue told Carly.

"That sounds good," Carly said, deciding not to even look at the menu.

"Coffee?" Maddie asked.

Betsy Sue and Carly nodded their heads.

"Where were we?" Betsy Sue asked after Maddie took back the menus and left the table.

Carly didn't want to return to the subject they'd been on, which had been Josh. "Were you and Maddie talking about Paulie Mitchell?"

"The one and only Paulie Mitchell. He and Maddie have been going together on and off for almost a year now. Off whenever Paulie gets cold feet. Maddie told him about a month ago not to call her again unless he made a real commitment to exploring what their relationship was all about."

Carly looked across the room at Maddie. She was taking an order from another table. "Maddie seems really nice and Paulie is a wonderful guy. Wouldn't it be great if they got married? We could do a wedding on the grounds. I think an outdoor wedding would be incredibly romantic."

"Speaking of romance..." Betsy Sue paused before she pitched the balance of her remark. "What is going on between you and Josh? I've noticed the way he looks at you."

"He doesn't look at me like anything." Carly shook her head because Betsy Sue's notion was entirely absurd. "He barely even looks at me when he's giving me riding lessons."

Carly pictured Josh sitting on the rail of the fence the way he did while she rode Lady Luck around, doing her utmost to get his full attention. It wasn't always easy to tell where he was looking because he usually wore dark sunglasses.

Carly elaborated on her point. "He hasn't even decided if he's comfortable having me for a partner."

"Really?" Betsy Sue remarked inconsequentially while she buttered a roll for herself.

"Yes." Carly sighed, then shook her head as Betsy Sue offered the bread basket. "The first night I was here he told me he wanted to buy me out."

"I can understand him feeling that way at first. He didn't know you. He had no way of judging what you were made of."

"I'm female. That's his main issue. He doesn't want a woman for a partner."

"I bet that has to do with him having had a bad marriage."

"Do you know anything about his marriage?" Carly tried to sound nonchalant.

"No." Betsy Sue bit into her roll, chewed, then added, "Anyway I'm sure he realizes by now that he doesn't have to worry about the two of you working well together." Betsy Sue had a half-concealed grin on her mouth. "I think the female part might even be working in your favor."

"You don't know about the stupid suggestion I made to him. I don't have anything working in my favor."

"What did you suggest?"

"That we should spend more money on advertising and push to expand the business. I had this idea in my head about trying to turn the show into something like a Disney World. I wasn't considering how many businesses fail because they overextend themselves."

Betsy Sue shrugged. "I don't have much of a business head. I do know that before Josh became your Uncle Bobby's partner the show was close to folding, and it wasn't that we weren't doing business. Your uncle was taking a lot of money out of the business and using it to play poker and there was a big bank note on the business at the time. When Josh came in he put your uncle on a gambling allowance and made Bobby stick to it. Josh also made sure that the money he invested as his share of the partnership went toward the bank note and not poker. Within a year Josh had the rest of the note paid off. Bobby was thrilled to get that noose lifted from around his neck. I'll tell you something else. Poquotte Falls couldn't handle a Disney World on their doorstep. Everyone enjoys a laid-back life-style here."

"It's a great life," Carly responded longingly.

"I know it takes some adjusting, coming from a big city. It took Tom some time to adjust to living in Poquotte and he was just from Tulsa."

"I haven't found it hard at all to adjust to a small town." She'd met Betsy Sue's husband, Tom, a few times. She liked him a lot. The two made a terrific couple.

"Poquotte Falls is a wonderful place to raise a family. We've been saving up. If Tom gets the promotion he's been pushing for, we're going to start trying."

Maddie brought over their lunch order. "How about the three of us getting together one night next week?" she asked.

"Definitely." Betsy Sue looked to Carly.

"Great," Carly said enthusiastically, liking the idea of making another friend.

"I'll call you and set it up," Betsy Sue told Maddie.

The waitress rushed off. The dining room was filling up.

"Did you tell Josh that you changed your mind about wanting to try and expand the business?" Betsy Sue asked as she began to eat.

"No." Absently, Carly poured honey-mustard sauce on her salad. "He'd only think I was saying it because I want him to accept our partnership."

"Is he still trying to buy you out?"

"He hasn't said anything about it recently, but that's because he's still giving me riding lessons."

"What does that have to do with it?"

"Umm . . ." Carly tried to remember how she'd felt when Josh had offered to take over her riding lessons. "I'm not sure." All she could remember clearly was how her pulse had raced when she'd danced with him. She hadn't had the same experience dancing with any of the other men on the ranch.

Betsy Sue put a slice of tomato on her fork and said, "I still say he's attracted to you. I'm sure he doesn't want to be, but he is. You've fallen for him, haven't you?"

"I have not fallen for him, and he is not attracted to me." She said it so stridently a couple of women close by turned their heads to stare at her.

Carly brought her voice down to a more conversational level. "One night last week I went to Mother's with the guys and he was going to come along, but he changed his mind when Paulie invited me to come. Every time I show up to help out with something he and the guys are doing, he shoos me away. And when he helps me dismount off Lady Luck he locks his elbows so that he can bring me down without any chance of our bodies touching. That's how attracted he is to me."

"Hmm," Betsy Sue said, then took time out to eat.

Carly picked up her fork and tried to do the same, but she was all worked up. She thought about how she'd expected him to offer to give her a massage again when he'd taken over her riding lessons. He hadn't, and she'd pretended to be all achy even after she'd stopped feeling sore.

"That just proves my point." Betsy Sue expanded on her "hmm" during a hiatus between bites. "I always say the more they fight, the harder they fall. What you're doing wrong is letting him off too easy."

"What should I do?" Carly realized as the question came out of her mouth that she was as good as conceding her feelings for Josh.

Betsy Sue smiled smugly.

Carly puckered her mouth. "Even if I am attracted to him, he isn't attracted to me."

"He isn't dating anyone," Betsy Sue informed her. "It's a small town. I would have heard about it. What he had with Alicia Marin was nothing."

"He could meet someone anytime now. Somewhere else besides Poquotte Falls. Maybe Tulsa." Carly conjured up an image of Alicia Marin. What if he did start dating again? What if he fell in love? God, he might even ask her to be in his wedding party. Then he'd have children and she'd be Auntie Carly....

"I don't see that you have anything to lose by testing my theory," Betsy Sue continued. "If you're right and he's not attracted to you, nothing is going to happen. If you're wrong, something is going to happen."

"Exactly how am I supposed to test your theory?" Carly didn't really believe for one minute that Betsy Sue was on to something. But what did she have to lose?

"You've got to be sexier with him. Not overt. You know what I mean."

"What? Bat my eyes?" Carly made a face. "I'm not the sexy type. I'm not good at it."

"I have an idea." Betsy Sue bubbled. "What if I called in sick tomorrow and you offer to do the skit with him? I could have laryngitis. Something like that."

"Oh, no! I couldn't." Carly rapidly shook her head.

"Yes, you could. I'll teach you the lines."

"It's not the lines. I know the lines."

"The costume will fit you. You're a little taller and thinner, but you'll have on boots and no one will notice that the pants are a bit short. You can use a safety pin to tighten the waist on the skirt. This is perfect.

You'll have an excuse to be as sexy as you want to be and it will be totally risk free."

"You're forgetting about what's out there," Carly argued.

"What's out where?"

"An audience. That's what's out there!"

"Just don't let yourself think about there being an audience. Think about the goal."

"I can't do it," Carly remonstrated. "If you call in sick, I still won't do it."

Betsy Sue wasn't listening. "Hurry up and eat. We have a lot of shopping to do. Your wardrobe needs an entire overhaul. You need Western boots. There's nothing like white Western boots and a short skirt. Definitely a male turn-on."

"Right." Carly rolled her eyes. "There's nothing like pointed white Western boots on my size-ten feet."

Betsy Sue grinned. "It's not the size of your feet he's going to be looking at when you perform the skit with him."

"I'm not doing the skit," Carly insisted. "Betsy Sue, please forget about it. Promise me."

"All right," Betsy Sue answered, but she had her fingers crossed.

Chapter Nine

"You're not wearing your new clothes," Betsy Sue scolded, coming into the mess hall the following morning.

Carly was at the sink cleaning up the dishes from the brunch Gabby put together on show days. The older man was tending to his herb garden out back.

Carly shut off the water and turned to Betsy Sue. "I haven't decided yet what I'm keeping and what's going back. Those very short shorts you talked me into are going back."

Betsy Sue grinned.

Just then Josh walked in and Betsy Sue immediately took the grin off her face and put her hand to her forehead. "I was just telling Carly that I'm not sure I can make it through today."

Carly blinked in shock and gaped at Betsy Sue.

Josh didn't notice the expression on Carly's face. His eyes were on Betsy Sue. "What's wrong?"

"I feel like I'm coming down with what Tom had a week ago. One of those twenty-four-hour bugs." Betsy Sue let one shoulder droop.

Carly looked up at the ceiling. She couldn't believe that Betsy Sue was pulling this on her.

"Come on. I'll drive you home," Josh said.

"I can drive myself home," Betsy Sue responded sluggishly. Then on a stronger note added, "Really."

"You're sure?" Josh wasn't convinced.

"I'm sure." The actress put more conviction in her voice. "I feel terrible leaving you in the lurch like this. I've never missed a show day before."

"Don't worry about it," Josh assured her. "Go home and take care of yourself. I'll give you a call later."

Betsy Sue headed for the door, surreptitiously mouthing to Carly, "Don't be a chicken," on her way out. Carly couldn't give Betsy Sue any indication of the aggravation she was feeling because Josh was watching her.

"You do have someone who can fill in for Betsy Sue, don't you?" Carly asked Josh nervously as soon as the other woman was out the door.

Josh's first thought had been to just drop the skit and fill in the space with more stunts and lasso tricks. That was quickly followed by another thought. An opportunistic thought.

"You'd fit into Betsy Sue's costume." Josh wasn't about to slam the door when opportunity came knocking.

After a second to catch her breath, Carly muttered, "I'm too tall...."

"You're not that much taller than Betsy Sue." Josh deliberately let his gaze travel up and down her body.

"There's got to be someone who would fit the costume better than I would." How in the world could she say lines in front of an audience? Not to mention the way she'd be dressed when she said those lines—her midriff bare and her legs showing.

"I guess I should know better than to expect you to be willing to give it a try." The problem Josh found with baiting her, the way he was baiting her, was that it made him feel like a second-rate bum.

Carly hated having him feel that she wasn't willing to even try. He was right to think that she wasn't pulling her fair share of this partnership—even if Betsy Sue had framed her.

This is it, Carly. Do it or forever be a chicken. "I'll do it," she told him.

"Forget it." He wasn't looking for her to actually do it. He was only out to make a point that this business wasn't for her.

"I said I'll do it." Carly had a sudden rush of adrenaline.

"You can't do it," Josh said impatiently, annoyed that she'd accepted his challenge. What was she thinking? She wouldn't be able to carry off the skit.

He knew how terrified she'd be. "You'll never be able to do it in front of an audience."

Carly's hazel eyes focused on Josh with determination. "I wouldn't offer to do it if I didn't feel I could. I *can* do it."

Denny walked in just then. "Hey, I heard the two of you outside the door. What's going on?"

Josh answered tersely, "Betsy Sue went home. She's not feeling well. Carly wants to play Calamity Jane."

"So what's the problem?" Denny asked.

Josh yanked in a breath. "She can't do it!"

Carly got even more fired up. "I can do it!"

"Well, I'm not doing it with you," Josh countered.

"Carly, if Josh doesn't want to do it with you, I'll do it with you," Denny butted in.

Carly and Josh both glared at Denny. It was Josh who spoke. "Since when did you take over running things here?"

"All I meant..." Denny backed down without finishing.

"You want to do this?" Josh returned his annoyed gaze to Carly. "You really want to do this?"

"Yes." She met his look fiercely. Only she was already losing some steam. If he hadn't just turned this into a battle of the sexes or a battle of wills—whatever it was he was calling it these days—she would have backed down.

"Do you want to run through it?" Josh asked tightly. She was driving him up a wall.

"I don't have to run through it. I know the lines."
Carly resolutely held her position. Doing it once, as
far as she was concerned, was already one time too
many.

Carly tried on the fringed shirt Betsy Sue wore as
Calamity Jane. Betsy Sue had rolled the cuffs to
shorten the sleeves. When Carly undid the folds she
found that the shirt fit fine.

She put on the pull-away pants, snapping them
closed. She set the waist so that the band was more on
her hips. The pants were still a little short, but not all
that bad with her brand-new white Western boots.

Carly practiced pulling off the pull-away pants. She
did it three times, snapping them in place, then pulling them off again.

Satisfied that she knew how to do it, Carly took off
the pants and shirt. She studied the midriff top and the
short skirt, which was to be worn underneath her re-
movable top layer. She was alone in the dressing room
Betsy Sue used on the second floor of the fake saloon. Everyone in the show knew she was making her
debut. They'd all given her words of encouragement,
including "break a leg."

What crazy person had invented that phrase?

Carly looked down at her uncoordinated legs. She
was clad only in the romantic pink satin bra and
panties that she'd bought in Tulsa at Betsy Sue's insistence. She hadn't really needed a push at all to also
buy a set in sensuous black satin and passionate va-

nilla satin. So much for having always thought that practical cotton lingerie held up best.

After a few deep breaths, Carly put on the skirt to the costume. She had a safety pin with her, but she didn't need it. Like the pants, the waist wasn't all that loose. She had been eating like a truck driver because of Gabby's great meals and all the fresh air her body hadn't been accustomed to. She might have noticed she'd put on some weight if there'd been a full-length mirror in the cabin. There was one in the dressing room. After putting on the studded and fringed midriff top, she walked over to take a look at herself.

Somehow in these past weeks, she'd become curvaceous. And she was a bit fuller on top than Betsy Sue. The top's material didn't pull, but it did cling.

Carly smiled naughtily and posed seductively in the mirror. Her self-admiration was interrupted by a knock on the closed door. Josh's voice called out, "Are you decent?"

"Yes." Carly's pulse took a huge leap.

Josh opened the door and froze. He felt a groan start somewhere deep in his body. He cleared his throat as it reached an avenue of escape.

Carly watched as Josh's gaze slowly raked her body. Though she'd tried to tell herself that Betsy Sue might be right about him being a little attracted to her, not once had she honestly believed it. Now she knew. She knew as a woman knows. She knew from his eyes that she needn't have worried about not having any sex appeal for him.

Didn't love follow attraction?

"What do you think?" Carly could hear her voice reach the exactly right tone between coyness and flirtatiousness.

"It fits," was Josh's response as he forced his eyes off her. He'd never before noticed how sexy that costume was. It hadn't looked all that sexy to him when Betsy Sue wore it. Of course, having Calamity Jane look sexy with her pants and shirt off *was* the whole point of the skit.

"The pull-away pants are a little short," Carly said, attempting to draw his focus back to her. When she was sure she had his attention, at least peripherally, Carly tilted her head and made her hair swing a little.

Josh noticed her hair, he'd been looking at it all morning. He realized she'd done something new. He liked it. He liked it a lot.

"These boots make the short pants less obvious," Carly said into the silence.

Josh looked down at her white Western boots and then dragged his eyes up her long shapely legs. Had that skirt always been so short?

Josh struggled for a comment and came up with, "Uh-huh."

"I guess I'd better put the pants and shirt on now." She gave him a very happy smile. "It's almost time for us to go on, isn't it?"

Josh nodded his head. It took a moment longer for him to put his feet into motion. "Well...I'll see you downstairs.... In the back."

He had his hand on the door as he turned his head to take one more look at her. What had ever happened to that schoolmarm-librarian demeanor of hers?

Paulie as Butch Cassidy and Ben as The Sundance Kid rode around to the back of the staged Western town where Carly and Josh were waiting for their cue. Carly sat in the box seat of the Pony Express, Josh on the horse he rode for the act. He'd switched the horse that usually pulled the Pony Express and hitched on Lady Luck. He knew Carly would be more at ease with that horse.

"How are you doing?" Josh asked, looking Carly over. He couldn't believe how relaxed she seemed to be. He, on the other hand, was a basket case.

"I'm fine." She was feeling pretty sure of herself on at least one count—the one that counted the most to her.

Carly had just enough time to catch a good-luck sign from Paulie and Ben as the announcer called out, "Here comes Calamity Jane bringing in the mail. Isn't that Wild Bill Hickok riding in after her?"

Holding her breath, Carly flicked the reins and Lady Luck moved forward, and then around to center stage. Out of the corner of her eye, Carly kept Josh in her sight as he rode beside the wagon.

For half a second Carly forgot to pull in the reins to halt Lady Luck. Then she yanked and brought the wagon to a stop.

Josh athletically dismounted from his horse, and Carly waited for him to say his line, but he didn't deliver it right off. Instead, his eyes found hers, and he gave her a soft and encouraging look—a personal moment of communication not meant for the crowd. The butterflies that had started having a heyday in her stomach relaxed to a flutter.

"Need a hand coming down, Calamity?" Josh drawled his line.

"I can get down all by myself." Carly tried her best to imitate Betsy Sue's Mae West drawl. *Don't think about the audience,* Carly ordered herself. "But I sure wouldn't want to spoil your reputation as a *gentleman.*"

Josh put his hands to Carly's waist. He gripped her firmly, possessively.

Carly tried looking into Josh's eyes as he brought her down and put her on her feet, but his focus had moved to the audience as he let go of her waist.

"So, Calamity, did you shoot any bad guys along the way?" Josh put the teasing tone in his voice that went with the question.

Carly placed her hands on her hips and pushed her chest out, causing Josh to swallow hard now that his eyes were back on her.

"Only about ten this time," Carly bragged. "Had to use two rifles. One in each hand."

"One in each hand," Josh repeated, tossing the audience a forced grin. He was thinking about her taking the pull-away pants and shirt off. He was thinking about her being ogled by the crowd. He was thinking about her being ogled by the guys.

Josh glanced over at Denny, Billy Jack, Paulie and Ben, who were all standing together at the sideline watching the skit.

"Don't you go sassing me, Wild Bill," Carly countered impudently. "That's no way to treat a lady."

"A lady!" Josh just managed part of a grin for the sake of the skit. "You sure don't look like any lady I've ever seen."

"I can look like a lady anytime I want to look like a lady," Carly retorted, playing her part to the hilt.

Josh considered ending the skit right now. He would have done it if he could have figured out a way to do so. Didn't she have enough sense in her head to know this kind of thing wasn't for her? How was she going to handle being whistled at? She blushed and got flustered when a guy just looked at her sideways.

"I'd have to see it to believe it." Josh got the line out after much too long a hesitation.

Pulling in a series of quick breaths, Carly took her shirt off and threw it into the buckboard of the wagon. She pulled off the pull-away pants next and did the same with them. They hadn't whipped off as easily as she'd been able to whip them off when she'd been practicing, but they had come off without all that much ado.

The audience broke into hoots, howls and whistles.

Carly could feel a flush come to her cheeks, but it was as much from knowing she was getting the right reaction from the crowd as it was from her innate shyness.

Josh took his jacket off and fanned his face. He wasn't just hamming it up for the crowd. He truly was breaking into a sweat.

Carly took a long deep breath and wiggled her hips in front of Josh. There were more hoots, howls and whistles, but the noise wasn't clearly registering on her now. She had her eyes glued on Josh, who had his eyes glued on her hips. It took Carly a few minutes to realize she had a line to say. Then just as she got the line into her mind, Josh changed the act. He took his jacket and firmly put it around her shoulders. The line flew right out of Carly's head. She stared at him mutely.

Josh couldn't believe what he'd just done, but he had, and there wasn't anything he could do about it now.

He took the lapels of his jacket in his hands and bent Carly forward to whisper the line to her.

Carly said it haltingly to his prompting. "Think-you-might-be-fixing-to-make-an-honest-woman-of-me-one-of-these-days?"

"Maybe one of these days," Josh replied by rote without his usual laugh to the crowd. "Right now that's not quite what I'm fixing to do."

Carly moved her feet at Josh's nudging. He practically hefted her into the wagon portion of the Pony Express and then leaped in himself.

Carly knew in some part of her mind that she was supposed to be concealed from the audience's view, but she was sitting and could see and be seen by the crowd. The bigger thought in Carly's head at this

point was that Josh had decided she hadn't been doing justice to the act at its most critical moment. She
hadn't said the line on time. She probably hadn't even
wiggled right. It was the only reasoning she could
come up with for him having thrown his jacket over
her.

"I'm sorry," he said tensely, sitting beside her.

Carly was about to shrug her shoulders in some attempt at making a face-saving response, but his hands
had already moved to her shoulders. Without much of
a push, he pressed her backward until she was prone
on the buckboard. He followed her down. Their
breaths mingled together as their faces met. He
prompted her to say the last line.

Carly raised her head and said it over Josh's shoulder. "Now I know why they call you *Wild* Bill." She
got it out louder than was necessary. The crowd had
gotten quiet.

The sounds came then. More hoots, howls and
whistles. Then the announcer's voice. "Thank you all
for coming. Tell your friends and come back soon."

Carly heard tom-toms and the wagon began to
move. Josh had rolled onto his back and wasn't looking at her. As soon as the wagon stopped moving, he
sprang to his feet.

"I'll get out, then I'll get you out," he said, his eyes
still avoiding her. He wasn't happy with himself.

Billy Jack, Denny, Ben and Paulie were all in the
back now. Before Josh had a chance to assist Carly,
Denny was helping her down.

"You were terrific," Denny said, smiling brightly. "Paulie has plans for tonight, but the rest of us are taking you to Mother's after dinner to celebrate."

Carly said a strained, polite "Thank you." With Josh's jacket still over her shoulders, she walked to the saloon to get out of Betsy Sue's costume.

Carly had just closed the door to the dressing room when the knock came. "I want to talk to you," Josh said from outside the door.

Carly pivoted and opened the door to him. "I don't need a pep talk," she told him, remaining at the threshold, not giving him permission to enter the room.

Josh ran one hand through his hair. "You've got the wrong idea in your head. You were terrific out there."

"Right," Carly said, raising her chin. "That's why you threw your jacket over me, because I had it right."

"You did have it right." Josh was thoroughly agitated. "You performed very well."

"Then why did you put your jacket over me?"

Josh bit his bottom lip in frustration. "I didn't want the guys gawking at you in that costume. You're the boss." He was in quicksand, sinking fast, trying to keep his head above ground.

In the flash of an instant Carly went from feeling utterly dejected to utterly thrilled. "Right." It wasn't the boss part of his remark that had thrilled her. He'd felt jealous. She was sure of it.

Josh turned and took off.

She stood looking after him, smiling.

* * *

Carly had no doubt that Josh was going to show up with the guys when they came to take her to Mother's. Only he wasn't in the lineup of motorcycles. There was just Denny, Ben and Billy Jack. It was Denny who got off his bike and approached her with his extra helmet.

"Hey, sweetheart, you are looking good." Denny smiled, giving her a thorough once-over.

"Thanks," Carly responded, unhappily going with the flow. She'd dressed to knock Josh's socks off. She was wearing a nicely fitted white polo under a black-and-white plaid flannel shirt that she'd left open down the front and tied jauntily at her waist. She had on her new white boots over nearly skintight black jeans.

Carly took the helmet from Denny and put it on. She wanted to ask where Josh was, but she didn't. She hadn't seen him since he'd come to the door of the dressing room. She'd opted to make herself something light to eat in the cabin, and hadn't joined the guys for one of Gabby's dinners. She'd talked excitedly to Betsy Sue by phone. Now she was going to have to change the report. Josh wasn't attracted to her. If he was attracted to her, he would have been here now.

"All set?" Denny asked as Carly fixed the strap of the helmet under her chin.

"Yes," Carly answered, then followed Denny to his bike. Josh Spencer could take a flying leap, Carly thought angrily to herself.

*   *   *

Josh sat in the mess hall inserting a few words here and there while Gabby kept up a steady stream of gab. Josh was only half-listening. He was thinking about Carly—thinking about her being out with Denny, Ben and Billy Jack. Mostly he was thinking about her being with Denny.

At ten p.m. Gabby yawned. "It's time for these tired bones to get to bed."

"See you in the morning," Josh said as Gabby rose to his feet.

Less than ten minutes later Josh was on his bike and heading for Mother's.

Carly was on the crowded dance floor with Denny when Josh walked into the bar. He picked Carly out right away—not a hard thing to do considering her red hair.

Ben broke a conversation he was having with a cute blonde at the bar as Josh walked by. "You decided to come?"

Not slowing his pace, Josh gave a nod of his head to the rhetorical question and kept walking. He negotiated his way onto the dance floor.

Carly didn't see Josh until he was directly behind Denny. Her heart flip-flopped. Denny was saying something to her, but the only answer he got was a tap on his shoulder from Josh.

"I'm cutting in," Josh said coolly, his eyes making it clear he was pulling rank.

Denny let out an irritated breath, but he dropped his arms from around Carly, and stepped grudgingly aside.

Josh fit Carly firmly into his embrace. Her hand came up to slip around his neck as she dissolved against him.

"Hi," Josh whispered against her hair.

"Hi," Carly breathlessly whispered back.

"Have you been dancing with Denny long?" he asked.

Tipping her head back, she said, "We just started dancing. We were playing pool before."

"Did you win?" Josh smiled at Carly.

"Three out of four." She gazed at him mischievously. "I let him win the first game when he thought he was showing me how to play."

Josh laughed and hugged her tighter.

Carly smiled at him sassily, then put her head back to his shoulder and dreamily closed her eyes. She didn't have to concentrate on her feet. Her body was moving perfectly with his.

The group of musicians ended the ballad and began another slow tune without a break. Josh took the hand he was holding down at her side and lifted it up to join her other hand around his neck. He caught her by the hips, sending tremors down Carly's body.

"You were incredible in the skit," he murmured in her ear.

"Really?"

"Really." His leg found its way between hers.

Three ballads later, Josh asked in a voice he could hear had gone husky on him, "Do you want to take a ride?"

Carly lifted her head off his shoulder and swung her eyes to his. "Yes."

They left Mother's without saying good-night to any of the guys.

Outside Josh gave Carly his extra helmet. She put it on while he put on his. She got on the bike behind him, wishing that they didn't have to wear helmets.

Josh rode out of town and pulled onto the highway in the opposite direction from the show's grounds. He didn't have any particular destination in mind, only that he didn't want to take her home and say good-night. Riding with the wind hitting his face was a relief. He'd been getting all heated up dancing with her. If she'd been anyone else he knew what he'd be angling to do now. But wanting Carly Gerard physically was no simple thing.

Josh slowed down some as he saw the Red Star Motel coming up, but he didn't stop. It took all the willpower he had not to stop and see what her reaction would be.

Carly looked over at the Red Star Motel as Josh drove by it. She'd thought he was going to pull in and was startled by how much she'd wanted him to.

Josh steered the bike to the side of the road. Motor still running—both the bike's and his—Josh checked the flow of traffic. A few cars whizzed by on either side. When it was clear, Josh banked the bike into a wide swing and headed back toward the turnoff to town. But he didn't take it when they got there.

Carly didn't want to believe the night was over, even as he pulled up in front of the cabin. He braked and she wondered if he was going to come inside with her. Every wayward dream and fantasy she'd had about him began to vie for her immediate attention.

Josh took his helmet off and strapped it to the bar of the bike.

With her heart causing a racket, Carly took her helmet off and handed it to him.

Carly got off the bike on teetering legs. She'd got very good at being a temptress with him in her dreams. But she didn't have that kind of confidence in herself for real.

She stood motionless, trying to get her breathing to calm down. It was dark, but she had put the porch light on earlier. She could see him clearly enough.

Josh got off the bike and paced a few steps. "I know I told you that I don't have a problem about mixing business with pleasure, but I was lying. It's a lousy mix."

Carly chewed her bottom lip.

Josh let his head droop forward and shook it in a slow gesture of exasperation. "You really should go back to New York."

Carly was about to rebut his remark, but his arm had come around her waist. Before she could get a word out, his mouth was on hers.

Hot and untamed as the kiss was, it didn't last long. Josh withdrew as quickly as he'd begun, leaving Carly flooded with confusion.

"Good night, Carly," he told her brusquely. "Think about what I said."

Carly watched Josh get back on his bike and take off. He wasn't heading to the bunkhouse. He was leaving the grounds. Carly thought about what he'd said about wanting her to go back to New York. Then she thought about how Betsy Sue had told her. "The more they fight, the harder they fall." Carly liked that last thought a lot better.

Chapter Ten

Carly reined in Lady Luck and prepared for Josh to assist her in dismounting. It had taken her almost a week since the night when he'd shown up at Mother's to get him to give her any personal attention. He'd begged off her riding lessons every morning saying he had something he needed to do or needed to check on for the show. But today was Monday and there was no show. Even at that, she hadn't been able to corner him until after lunch.

Josh pushed off the fence where he'd been leaning and came up to her. Taking off his sunglasses, he said, "I think it's time that you tried dismounting on your own. I've shown you how to do it the right way. I'll catch you if you have a problem."

Josh thought his frustration level was about to crash

its limits. He'd been doing everything he could think of in order to not spend any time with her.

"I don't feel ready." Carly's gaze avoided the provoking insistence in his eyes. She'd already dismounted on her own a few times when he hadn't been around just to prove to herself that she could do it. Doing it in front of him meant the end of her lessons.

"If you're not ready yet, then I haven't done a good job. I'll get Billy Jack to continue with you." What ever had possessed him to take over her riding lessons from Billy Jack to begin with? Where had his head been?

Carly wanted to gnash her teeth, but she didn't. Instead, she dismounted from Lady Luck, doing it the right way, coming down backward not sideways.

Josh winked his approval as if he'd just scored some big point. "Now, don't you feel good?"

"Just terrific." This time Carly did gnash her teeth.

"Well, I'll see you," Josh said, taking Lady Luck's reins to walk the filly back to the stable.

"Do you have something to do today?" Carly asked, detaining him.

"I have to go to town. Pick up some things for Gabby."

Carly thought quickly. "I need some things in town. You don't mind if I go with you, do you?"

"Why don't you write out a list?" Josh countered. "I'll pick up what you need."

"I need things from the drugstore." Carly dropped her eyes to the ground, intending to give him the impression that she was embarrassed.

It worked. Josh got the message. "How soon can you be ready?"

"A half hour." Carly raised her eyes innocently.

"Okay," Josh responded, none too nicely.

Yes. Yes. Yes. Carly thought to herself.

Some thirty minutes later, Josh brought the Jeep around to the front of the cabin. She was waiting for him. Changing out of the loose jeans and shirt she'd been wearing to ride Lady Luck, she'd donned tight black jeans that rode low on her hips and a white sleeveless top that ended an inch or so above her wide leather western belt, displaying some of her skin that hadn't taken to the sun yet.

"Not many guys are as punctual as you are," Carly complimented him. "It's a very nice quality."

"Uh-huh," Josh grunted. He had no problem at all deciphering the outline of her fabulous long legs as she raised her feet and climbed in on the passenger side.

Carly fastened her seat belt and stretched out her legs comfortably. She'd been in the Jeep a number of times now. Once with Ben, twice with Paulie and a couple of times with Billy Jack at the wheel.

Josh drove out of the grounds and onto the road. He searched his mind for a topic of conversation—anything to keep from thinking about her legs and the couple of inches or so of skin he hadn't seen since she'd been in Betsy Sue's costume. "How's that new bookkeeping system you said you were working on?"

"It's working out." Carly smiled, catching his fleeting gaze. "When we get back, why don't you come in and I'll show you what I've been doing?"

"I have some things to do when we get back. I'll take a look first chance I get." Josh made his response as ambiguous as he could.

"You've been very busy lately. Isn't there something that I can be doing to help out?"

"You do enough." How much crazier did she want to make him?

Carly noted the tense set of his jaw. "You still don't feel that our partnership is going to work out. That's it, isn't it?"

Josh turned his head and met her eyes. "It's *not* going to work out."

Carly bit her bottom lip. "I know you still think we're on different wavelengths about the way the business should be run, but we're not anymore. I agree that we shouldn't be looking to expand. And I'm not just saying that to be agreeable. I mean it."

"Whether you mean it or not is not the point," Josh responded restlessly.

"What is the point?" Carly pressed.

Josh flashed her a vexed glance and then pulled off the road, bringing the Jeep to a stop on grass just over the breakdown lane. He turned his body fully toward her. "You want the point?"

"Yes." Carly didn't let herself flinch as she met his glare.

"The attraction between us is the point." His eyes were still locked with hers, but the look she was giv-

ing him back now was brand-new. Thoroughly provocative. A look that made Josh catch his breath.

Her stomach a million jittery nerves, Carly unfastened her seat belt. She turned to him fully. "I don't
see anything wrong with us being attracted to each
other."

Putting her hand on his shoulder for balance, Carly
placed her lips against his in an awkward attempt at a
kiss. She wasn't used to taking this kind of initiative.

When he made no move to help her out at all, Carly
lifted her head to see his face. "You don't want there
to be attraction between us. Is that it?"

Josh didn't answer.

Defeated, Carly hopelessly straightened herself in
her seat. She could feel herself blushing.

"Listen to me," Josh said tightly, wrestling with his
body and his conscience. "I'm completely burned out
on the entire concept of love. I know you want to be
sensible. There isn't going to be anything sensible
about this."

Carly absorbed what he was saying. What had being sensible about love ever gotten her? Certainly not
what she was feeling now.

She looked over at him. He couldn't be turned off
love. He just couldn't be. No one got turned off love.

"Do you want to sleep with me?" Josh questioned,
his eyes drilling into hers.

"What?" Carly was immediately ruffled not only
by the bluntness of his question, but also by the cheeky
tone he'd used in asking it.

"Do you want to sleep with me?" Josh repeated in the same manner as he'd asked the first time.

Furiously, Carly turned her head away.

"Is that a no?" Josh kept his voice glib.

"No," Carly answered precisely and started to get out of the Jeep. But his hands came out then to grip her waist. He lifted her and suddenly she was over the gearshift and sitting on his lap.

"This conversation isn't over," Josh said while Carly pushed against him, trying unsuccessfully to get away.

"I don't want to hear anything more from you."

Josh managed to get both her hands in one of his. He put his other hand into her hair and then he kissed her hard.

"Josh," Carly moaned helplessly when he removed his lips.

He kissed her again, this time seductively. Carly couldn't fight off what he made her feel. She couldn't even put up a token resistance against the longing that swept through her. Her mouth melded to his in response and he let go of her hands. Carly found his shoulders and held on.

The honk of not one, but a few, motorists passing by caused Carly and Josh to jerk apart. Flustered and clumsy, Carly moved herself, one leg at a time, over the console and back to her own seat.

Josh shook his head. "I feel like a damn teenager. I'm too old for making out in a car."

Carly heard what sounded like a grin in his voice before she turned her head to see one on his mouth.

Flustered and all, Carly smiled back.

"Of course, even a teenager would know better than to just pull to the side of the road in broad daylight," Josh quipped, not wanting to get back into the angry mood he'd been in before he'd kissed her.

"Do you think the people who honked could have been people that have seen the show? Or people who know us from around here?" Carly asked, trying to parry with him. The second kiss he'd given her still filled her senses.

"Considering the Jeep's got the lettering of the show on both hoods, it couldn't be bad for business." The smile Josh gave Carly was a kidding one.

"True." Carly grinned.

Josh put the Jeep in gear and pulled back onto the road. "I guess we didn't resolve anything. Did we?"

When she looked over at him, he gave her a sexy wink. "I don't think so," Carly rejoined, then couldn't hold back an edge of seriousness. "I guess you still want me to go back to New York?"

There was a part of him that did. He was split in half on the question. "I guess I've been pretty much a heel." He gave her a true evaluation of how he felt putting both parts of himself together.

"I don't know," Carly said softly. "I kind of like the battle of the sexes we've got ourselves into."

Josh flicked Carly a grin and they both noticed a sign advertising the Red Star Motel. "I could drive over there and we can go another round," Josh teased sexily. He wasn't entirely teasing, though he knew it wasn't going to happen right now. Of course, it happened almost every night when he closed his eyes.

"I think I stand a better chance of scoring points in public and in broad daylight," Carly bantered. She didn't want just sex with him, even if it was downright impossible to keep that in her mind when he was kissing her.

Josh angled his head and gave her an outrageous look. "Sweetheart, I'd be totally at your mercy in bed."

Carly sought a diversion and was glad to be presented by one since they'd just arrived in town. "Should I start looking for a parking place?" The heat on her cheeks was a clear indication that his remark had triggered the reaction he wanted.

"Okay." Josh grinned, feeling a whole lot better than he'd felt in a long time—counting from the time she'd arrived. He didn't have to fight off being attracted to her. His conscience was clear. She knew where he stood. He was interested in having sex with her, he wasn't interested in falling in love. It was now up to her how she wanted to handle him.

Not able to find a parking spot anywhere near the drugstore, Josh double-parked. He hadn't planned on going inside with her anyway.

"How long do you need?" he asked as she got out of the Jeep.

"Fifteen...twenty minutes." She didn't really need anything in particular from the drug store. Carly decided she'd look at some makeup and pick up some magazines. "How long will it take you to get what Gabby needs?"

"Not long." Josh had checked, but Gabby hadn't needed anything from town. He figured he'd browse around Durango's, a clothing store that carried Western apparel.

Carly went into the drugstore. Josh drove off for Durango's.

Carly had to wait a few minutes outside the drugstore before Josh came back. She'd bought a new shade of lipstick and three magazines that featured articles on how to get your man to fall in love with you. She was positive he wanted her body, but she was determined to get his heart.

Carly walked to the Jeep, which Josh had once again double-parked. She saw an expression on his face that she wasn't able to interpret. Then she saw a box on the passenger seat.

"It's for you," Josh said, still looking enigmatic.

Carly's eyes lit up. "You bought me something?"

"Uh-huh." Josh smiled, and because she was still standing at the side of the Jeep all astonished, he added, "Get in and you can open it up."

Carly tossed her bag of goodies in the back of the Jeep. She picked up the box, got in and put the box on her lap.

"Put your seat belt on," Josh ordered with his smile broadening at the look of anticipation on her face.

Carly fixed her seat belt in place. Josh worked the shift and clutch.

Carly stared down at the box. Her heart was racing.

"Aren't you going to open it?" Josh asked, after a minute.

Carly didn't need any further encouragement. Untying the bow, she raised the lid and pushed aside some tissue paper. "It's a Western hat!" Carly turned her excited eyes to Josh.

"Take it out and put it on." Josh smiled. "You can't be a real cowgirl without the right hat."

With shaky hands, but utmost care, Carly took the hat out of the box. It was a light shade of tan with a red band. Gingerly, Carly put it on her head. She didn't know what meaning she was supposed to read into his gift. But whatever it meant, she felt great.

Josh reached over with one hand and tilted it properly for her. "Does it fit?"

"Yes," Carly murmured.

"The band matches your hair. That's why I picked it. I like your hair."

"You do?" Carly didn't know what to say.

"Yes." Josh smiled slowly, sexily.

"Thank you for the hat." Carly leaned toward him, and though the brim of the hat made it a bit difficult, she was able to place a kiss on his jaw.

"You're welcome." He touched his finger to the spot where her mouth had just been. "Thanks for the thank-you."

"You're welcome," Carly quipped and tried to get a look at herself in the rearview mirror without being obvious.

Josh turned the mirror to face more her way.

Carly grinned.

Josh winked.

"Now that you've mastered acting and riding, we're going to have to find a new challenge for you," Josh said while Carly looked at herself in the mirror.

Carly gave him her gaze. "Maybe you can teach me how to drive this Jeep. I know how to drive, but not a stick shift."

"Sure. I'll give you your first lesson when we get back to the grounds."

Carly sat back, pleased that she'd come up with a reason for him to stick around her.

Josh drove relaxed, glad to have an excuse to spend time with her.

Paulie, Ben, Billy Jack and Denny were outdoors polishing their bikes when Josh pulled into the grounds.

Paulie was the first to comment on Carly's hat. "Hey, what have we got here?" he called over to Carly.

"A cowgirl," Carly rejoined.

Josh said with a grin, "This cowgirl is about to learn how to drive the Jeep. She needs a new challenge."

Ben ribbed, "Give us a chance to take cover first."

"Thanks for the vote of confidence," Carly retorted, laughing as she got out on her side while Josh got out from behind the wheel.

Putting aside their polishing for the moment, the men turned to watch Carly and Josh begin the lesson.

Carly didn't have to adjust the seat any with her long legs. She did wiggle some trying to settle in. She glanced at Josh. "You are going to keep your foot near the brake. Right?"

Josh put his hand out, and raised Carly's chin, and placed a kiss on her mouth. "That's for confidence," he whispered to her with a smile. It wasn't the only reason he'd just kissed her. He wanted the guys to know he was laying claim. Whether it got him anywhere or not, he didn't want there to be any mistake about that.

Chapter Eleven

A few days later, Carly was busily picking rosemary from Gabby's garden when she heard voices coming from the nearby stable. She hadn't intended to eavesdrop until she heard Paulie mention her name.

"Did Carly go with Josh to Tulsa?" Paulie asked.

"No," Ben answered. "I heard her say she had some bookkeeping she needed to get done to be ready for Jimmy Blatts's visit tomorrow."

"Have you seen the way those two have been tight as peas in a pod since last Monday?" Ben asked.

"I've seen it, and I don't like it," Paulie responded.

"Aren't you and Maddie an item again?"

"We're an item again. That woman has me just about hog-tied."

Lady Luck neighed and Carly could hear Ben soothe the animal. "So what's your issue with Carly and Josh?" Ben asked, once the horses had calmed down.

"What he's doing to Carly stinks. That's my issue."

"What are you talking about?"

Paulie replied sharply, "You know how he didn't want a female partner...."

"Right," Ben cut in.

"This is his newest plan to get her to sell out to him," Paulie went on.

"He's chasing after her because he wants her to sell out to him?"

"He wants her to fall for him. He wants her to think he's fallen for her. Then he breaks her heart by telling her that he hasn't fallen for her. She sells out to him and leaves."

Ben's voice rose in anger. "Did he tell you that was his plan?"

"It's obvious," Paulie responded. "What really burns me up is that she's such a sweetheart."

"She's a doll," Ben agreed.

Carly straightened up from where she'd been kneeling. She'd heard enough. Dropping the rosemary she'd already picked, Carly took off and ran to the cabin.

The tears came as soon as she was inside.

* * *

"What did you say about the warranty on this one?" Josh asked, having lost the thread of the salesman's pitch. His thoughts kept shifting to Carly.

"I said this one has the best warranty you're going to get," the gray-haired man repeated, pushing back in place the glasses he wore that kept sliding down his nose. "Six years on parts instead of the usual five years. Two years on labor and parts."

"Sounds good," Josh said, wanting to make as quick work as possible out of choosing a new rider mower, without abandoning his common sense. "What's the downside?"

"It's got a little less horsepower than some of the others. But you're not going to notice it."

Josh looked the machine over, but his mind was back on Carly. Unconsciously, a smile lifted the corner of his mouth. He thought about her confessing yesterday how scared she'd been just riding in the Jeep when she'd first arrived. Now she was driving the Jeep like a hellcat on wheels.

"Why don't you try out the seat?" the salesman suggested.

Josh ran his hand over the smooth leather, but his thoughts were still on Carly. He couldn't believe he hadn't yet tried to go as far with her as he ached to go. He could tell she was still a bit shy with him and a little self-conscious. Even more, she was hesitant and nervous. Yet at the same time she didn't disguise that she wanted him—would have let him take her anyplace he wanted to go.

Josh swung onto the seat. It was her hesitation that was keeping him in check, he realized. He wanted her trust as much as he wanted her body. He wanted to know that the trust was still going to be in her eyes after he made love to her.

Josh smiled inwardly. *Are you sure you should still be calling yourself a cowboy?*

It was four-thirty when Josh stopped the Jeep outside of the cabin. He expected that Carly would be inside, probably with her head in the books. He didn't intend for her to work any more today. He'd decided on his way back from Tulsa to take her for an early dinner and then to a movie. He'd never taken her on a real date before. He was getting a new surge of emotions where she was concerned. He didn't have them quite squared away, but the image of her beguiling face filled his mind as he pictured her hair, her eyes and her smile. He felt a breath-stopping sense of anticipation. The excitement at just the thought of being with her—at doing even simple, ordinary things together—was irrepressible.

Josh saw the suitcases the second he walked into the living room. The next thing he focused on was Carly. She was standing across the room, staring out a window.

When she realized he was in the room, she turned and crossed her arms stiffly in front of her. Josh glanced at her suitcases again before searching out her face.

Carly answered the question before he asked it. "I've decided I've had it with the Wild West."

He heard the sound of weariness in her voice before the words actually registered and it took a second longer for any reaction to set in.

"Would you mind telling me what brought this decision on?" Suddenly he was angry.

"I don't see the need to go into it." Her lids quivered. She was not going to cry. She refused to have him see her tears.

"Well, *I* see the need to go into it." His voice was tense.

"I know your plan." Carly looked away in a vain attempt to keep him from seeing the moisture in her eyes. "Let's just say I'm saving you the effort of having to see it through. I'll have my lawyer—" she didn't have a lawyer "—contact your lawyer and arrange for a settlement on the partnership."

"What plan?" Josh asked tersely.

"Oh, I've forgotten. You probably are your own lawyer." Carly marched over to her luggage, turning her back to him. She had a car coming to take her to the airport at five-fifteen.

Josh walked up to her, took her by the arm and swung her around none too gently. "I want an answer from you," he demanded. "What plan?"

Carly yanked free of his grip. "The plan to get me to fall in love with you by convincing me you've fallen in love with me. That plan!"

"I've never made a secret about wanting to get you in bed." Was she suddenly thinking of herself as a notch on his belt? Was that what brought this on? Josh pushed his hand through his hair. "Will you stay if I stop trying to seduce you?" He hadn't anticipated the emptiness he was feeling at the idea of her actually going. He didn't want her to leave.

"No." Tears were welling in her eyes.

"Why not? You like it here. You like being a part of this business. That suggestion you had about a souvenir shop is a good one. We can have a real partnership, Carly. I promise."

Carly couldn't swallow. She had a huge lump in her throat. Then like a floodgate that had been pushed on too hard, the dam burst open. The tears flowed in rivulets down her cheeks.

Josh wrapped his arms around her. "Stay," he whispered pleadingly.

"I can't." But she couldn't keep from leaning into him.

"Why not?" He held her tighter.

"Because I'm in love with you." She said the words with her face raised to him and her body trembling.

"What if I'm in love with you?" He put his mouth to one of her cheeks, tasting her salty tears. There wasn't any "what if" about it. He just hadn't figured it out till now.

"You're not." Carly sighed deeply, denying the possibility.

"You're wrong." He kissed away the tears on her other cheek, found some at the sides of her mouth and took care of those too.

"You're burned out on love," Carly reminded him, her gaze locked to his.

His eyes teased her. "You started a new flame. Talk about burning."

"Please don't do this to me...." She was holding on to him so tightly she wasn't sure she was still standing on her own power.

"Don't do what? Don't love you? I can't help it." He smiled into her face and then he kissed her, trying to convince her of the depth of emotion coursing through him.

Carly's eyes opened slowly as he raised his mouth from hers. She couldn't believe it. How could he have fallen in love with Carly Gerard, little bookkeeper from New York City?

"This isn't just a..." Her speech faltered.

"A seduction?" Josh grinned, finishing for her. "I've got more of a plan in mind than that."

"What plan?" Carly pulled away.

"To get you to marry me." His eyes met hers tenderly, then turned sexy. "I might even hold out until then."

Carly dived against him, throwing her arms around his neck. "Did you really just ask me to marry you?" She was overwhelmed.

"You've got the question right." Josh grinned.

Carly kissed him then, and there wasn't any hesitation, awkwardness or nervousness associated with it. When she took her mouth from his, her eyes were as provocative as a siren's.

"Would you really be at my mercy in bed?" Her voice was sultry and teasing.

"If you say yes to marrying me, you'll get to find out."

"Yes," Carly said quickly. She had tears in her eyes again, but they were good tears. They were very happy tears. They were the tears of a biker chick, cowgirl and bride-to-be.

They were the tears of a soon-to-be Wild West wife.

*   *   *   *   *

HE'S NOT JUST A MAN, HE'S ONE OF OUR

FATHER BY MARRIAGE
Suzanne Carey

Investigator Jake McKenzie knew there was more to widowed mom Holly Yarborough than met the eye. And he was right—she and her little girl were *hiding* on her ranch. Jake had a job to do, but how could he be Mr. Scrooge when this family was all he wanted for Christmas?

Fall in love with our Fabulous Fathers!

Coming in December, only from

Silhouette
R O M A N C E™

MILLION DOLLAR SWEEPSTAKES (III)

No purchase necessary. To enter, follow the directions published. Method of entry may vary. For eligibility, entries must be received no later than March 31, 1996. No liability is assumed for printing errors, lost, late or misdirected entries. Odds of winning are determined by the number of eligible entries distributed and received. Prizewinners will be determined no later than June 30, 1996.

Sweepstakes open to residents of the U.S. (except Puerto Rico), Canada, Europe and Taiwan who are 18 years of age or older. All applicable laws and regulations apply. Sweepstakes offer void wherever prohibited by law. Values of all prizes are in U.S. currency. This sweepstakes is presented by Torstar Corp., its subsidiaries and affiliates, in conjunction with book, merchandise and/or product offerings. For a copy of the Official Rules send a self-addressed, stamped envelope (WA residents need not affix return postage) to: MILLION DOLLAR SWEEPSTAKES (III) Rules, P.O. Box 4573, Blair, NE 68009, USA.

EXTRA BONUS PRIZE DRAWING

No purchase necessary. The Extra Bonus Prize will be awarded in a random drawing to be conducted no later than 5/30/96 from among all entries received. To qualify, entries must be received by 3/31/96 and comply with published directions. Drawing open to residents of the U.S. (except Puerto Rico), Canada, Europe and Taiwan who are 18 years of age or older. All applicable laws and regulations apply; offer void wherever prohibited by law. Odds of winning are dependent upon number of eligibile entries received. Prize is valued in U.S. currency. The offer is presented by Torstar Corp., its subsidiaries and affiliates in conjunction with book, merchandise and/or product offering. For a copy of the Official Rules governing this sweepstakes, send a self-addressed, stamped envelope (WA residents need not affix return postage) to: Extra Bonus Prize Drawing Rules, P.O. Box 4590, Blair, NE 68009, USA.

SWP-S1195

HAPPY HOLIDAYS!

Silhouette Romance celebrates the holidays with
six heartwarming stories of the greatest gift of all—
love that lasts a lifetime!

#1120 *Father by Marriage*
by Suzanne Carey

#1121 *The Merry Matchmakers*
by Helen R. Myers

#1122 *It Must Have Been the Mistletoe*
by Moyra Tarling

#1123 *Jingle Bell Bride*
by Kate Thomas

#1124 *Cody's Christmas Wish*
by Sally Carleen

#1125 *The Cowboy and the Christmas Tree*
by DeAnna Talcott

COMING IN DECEMBER FROM

Silhouette ROMANCE™

Silhouette

SPECIAL EDITION™

Holiday Elopements

He was a miracle Christmas baby....

It may have been more than luck that brought
Mariah Bentley to the aid of a child in distress. And
when she met the babe's attractive and available
uncle, Aaron Kerr, it soon looked as if Christmas
wedding bells would ring!

Don't miss
THE BRIDE AND THE BABY
(SE #999, December)
by Phyllis Halldorson

It's a

Holiday Elopements

—the season of loving gets an added boost with a
wedding. Catch the holiday spirit and the bouquet!
Only from Silhouette Special Edition!

It's our 1000th Special Edition and we're celebrating!

Join us these coming months for some wonderful stories in a special celebration of our 1000th book with some of your favorite authors!

Diana Palmer   Nora Roberts
Debbie Macomber   Christine Flynn
Phyllis Halldorson   Lisa Jackson

Plus miniseries by:

Lindsay McKenna, Marie Ferrarella, Sherryl Woods and Gina Ferris Wilkins.

And many more books by special writers!

And as a special bonus, all Silhouette Special Edition titles published during Celebration 1000! will have **_double_** Pages & Privileges proofs of purchase!

Silhouette Special Edition...heartwarming stories packed with emotion, just for you! You'll fall in love with our next 1000 special stories!

COMING NEXT MONTH

#1120 FATHER BY MARRIAGE—Suzanne Carey
Fabulous Fathers
Holly Yarborough was just another assignment, but that didn't
stop Jake McKenzie from falling for the sexy female rancher.
When Holly learned the truth, would Jake lose his new bride?

#1121 THE MERRY MATCHMAKERS—Helen R. Myers
Read Archer's children wanted a new mother and Marina Davidov
was perfect. Little did they know that years ago, she had broken
his heart—could Read give their love a second chance?

#1122 IT MUST HAVE BEEN THE MISTLETOE—
Moyra Tarling
In a long-ago night of passion, Mitch Tennyson had transformed
Abby Roberts's world. Now Mitch was back, and Abby felt
forgotten love mixing with the fear that he could learn the true
identity of her son....

#1123 JINGLE BELL BRIDE—Kate Thomas
Matt Walker needed a wife—fast. And sassy waitress
Annie Patterson seemed to fit the bill. With his cowboy charm
he won her hand. Could she find a way to lasso his heart?

#1124 CODY'S CHRISTMAS WISH—Sally Carleen
All Cody wanted for Christmas was a daddy—and a baby brother!
Would Ben Sloan be the right man for his mommy, Arianna? Only
Santa knew for sure!

#1125 THE COWBOY AND THE CHRISTMAS TREE—
DeAnna Talcott
Crystal Weston had an ideal marriage—until tragedy tore it apart.
Now her husband, Slade, had returned to town, determined to win
her back. But would the handsome cowboy still want to renew
their vows once he met the son he'd never known?

You're About to Become a *Privileged Woman*

Reap the rewards of fabulous free gifts and benefits with proofs-of-purchase from Silhouette and Harlequin books

Pages & Privileges™

It's our way of thanking you for buying our books at your favorite retail stores.

Pages & Privileges™

Harlequin and Silhouette—
the most privileged readers in the world!

For more information about Harlequin and Silhouette's PAGES & PRIVILEGES program call the Pages & Privileges Benefits Desk: 1-503-794-2499

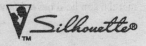
Silhouette®

SR-PP70